WHO ARE YOU?

MYSTERIES BY JOAN LOWERY NIXON

WHO ARE YOU?

—— // ——

JOAN LOWERY NIXON

DELACORTE PRESS

Published by
Delacorte Press
a division of Random House, Inc.
1540 Broadway
New York, New York 10036

Library of Congress Cataloging-in-Publication Data
Nixon, Joan Lowery.
      Who are you? / by Joan Lowery Nixon.
            p.   cm.
      Summary: When the police discover that a man who has
been shot has been keeping a file of her entire life, sixteen-year-
old Kristi, an aspiring artist, suspects a connection with the
possible theft of a painting from a museum.
      ISBN 0-385-32566-5
      [1. Art appreciation—Fiction. 2. Artists—Fiction.
3. Museums—Fiction. 4. Mystery and detective stories.] I. Title.
PZ7.N65Wgf   1999
[Fic]—dc21   98-43000
                                                                    CIP
                                                                    AC

The text of this book is set in 12-point Goudy.

Book design by Trish P. Watts

Manufactured in the United States of America

June 1999

10   9   8   7   6   5   4   3   2

BVG

for Karen Collins-Eiland
a dear friend

CHAPTER ONE

———— // ————

The doorbell rings, but Mom, Dad, and I just stare at each other. We've been building walls of angry words, slathering them over with shouts of "That's a completely unreasonable request!" and "You don't even try to understand!" and "Use your brain, Kristi! Do you think we're made of money?" and "You don't know anything about me. You don't care!"

The loud chime of the doorbell intrudes and suddenly we're silent. The noise is a shock, like being caught naked in the shower room after gym class. Dad clears his throat, turns, and walks to open the door.

I can see a short, auburn-haired woman, wearing a plain navy blue suit and white blouse. She faces

Dad on the doorstep. A tall, broad-shouldered man with a craggy, weather-beaten face stands behind her. He's wearing a dark blue suit and white shirt too.

"Are you Mr. Drew Evans?" the woman asks.

"Yes," Dad answers.

She holds out a small leather folder. Now I can see the glint of metal. It looks like a badge. "Sergeant Janice Nims. HPD homicide detective," she says. She nods toward the man with her. "This is Sergeant Jerry Balker, my partner. May we come in?"

"Why, yes," Dad says as he opens the door wide. His voice cracks and gets strangely high and tight as he asks, "What's happened? What's wrong? Is something the matter?"

Mom and I come to life, bumping into each other, trying to make way as the detectives follow Dad into the living room.

"Please sit down. Here . . . no, here," Mom says. She smoothes down her dark brown hair, fluffs pillows, and attempts to make a soft drink can disappear, while I scoop up a pile of my books and homework papers.

Dad has himself under control now, and he says, "Detectives Nims and Balker, this is my wife, Callie, and our daughter, Kristin."

We shake hands and murmur greetings, perching on chairs while we wait for what will come next. Although Sergeant Balker has a kind, pleasant look in his eyes, Sergeant Nims studies me as though she's trying to memorize me for a test, and it makes me uncomfortable. Why should two homicide detectives visit our family on a Sunday morning?

Sergeant Nims leans forward in her chair. A notepad and pen appear in her hands. Did they suddenly arrive by magic, or haven't I been paying attention? "Are you acquainted with a man named Douglas Merson?" she asks.

Dad and Mom look at each other blankly. "Mersome?" Mom questions.

"Merson," Sergeant Nims corrects her. "Douglas Merson." She glances at me, but I just shrug.

Dad shakes his head, and Mom answers, "No. Who is he?"

Sergeant Nims doesn't respond to Mom's question. Instead, she says, "We have reason to believe that he's acquainted with your family." Again she gives me a strange, searching look. Why? I never heard of this Douglas Merson.

"Merson? Merson?" Mom starts thinking aloud. "Maybe we met through our church? Or the high school? Is he in the booster club at Carter High? Tall man? Has a son on the football team?"

"No," Sergeant Balker says. His words are a slow, comfortable drawl compared to Sergeant Nims's staccato bursts. "Douglas Merson's home is in River Oaks, and his son is no longer living."

"Then I doubt if I've met his wife . . ."

"Merson's not married now."

Dad suddenly sits upright. "Wait a minute," he says. "Douglas Merson. I knew that name sounded familiar. It was on the television news last night and in this morning's *Houston Chronicle*. He was robbed and shot yesterday evening at the front door of his house. Isn't that right?"

Mom gasps. "He was murdered?"

"Fortunately, Mr. Merson didn't die," Sergeant Balker answers. "He was shot twice—once in the shoulder and once in the jaw. He's in intensive care, but it looks like he'll make it." Balker turns to Dad, and for the first time I can see the intensity of his gaze. "Have you ever had any business dealings with Merson?"

"Not to my knowledge," Dad answers. "He's not one of my clients. I'm an accountant. My wife and I are both accountants. We have our own firm." Dad tries a smile that doesn't make it. "March . . . income taxes due soon. This is our busy season, you know."

"We know," Sergeant Nims says. *And we don't care,* her impatient tone implies. She goes on to question Dad and Mom about the name and address of their company and how many employees they have. It doesn't take long. There's only Betsy, their secretary and receptionist.

Again Sergeant Nims looks at me as though she can see right into and through me. I can't help squirming. I don't like it. No one's asked me any questions, but I blurt out, "We don't know this Douglas Merson you're talking about. We've never met him." I try to ease the situation with humor, as I add, "And we certainly didn't shoot and rob him, if that's what you're getting at." After I've said it, I realize it didn't come across as being funny.

Surprise flickers briefly in the sergeant's eyes, but

she keeps her gaze steadily on me. "We have reason to believe he *does* know you," she says. "Our officers were called to the house by a neighbor who heard gunshots. The door was open. It's possible that Mr. Merson opened the door to someone he knew."

I break in, irritated that she hasn't believed us. Also, I'm a little frightened. Does she really think one of us shot Mr. Merson? "I sometimes read the newspapers," I tell her, "and I nearly always listen to the evening news on TV. There's often something about 'Police report that there was no forced entry, so the victim must have opened the door to someone he knew.' But it's not true. People open doors to salesmen or repairmen or other people they don't know. Just because he opened the door doesn't mean—"

"Kristi, please." Mom touches my arm, and I close my mouth, damming up the spill of words.

Sergeant Nims continues. I listen carefully, even though I can't stand her calmness. I hate her for frightening and upsetting us, then acting so cool about the whole thing.

"Mr. Merson was lying in the entry hall. His watch was gone. We were told he was in the habit of wearing it. After the paramedics took him to Ben Taub Hospital, we searched the immediate vicinity of the house for evidence connected to the crime. On the table in the living room was an open folder. We assume Mr. Merson had been going through the items in the folder, so we intend to follow up. We're very much interested in the contents of the folder."

As she pauses, Dad waits patiently. I clamp my

5

lips together, refusing to ask the obvious question, but Mom's curiosity gets the best of her. She asks, "What was in the folder?"

"Newspaper clippings," the detective says. "A birth announcement from the *Chronicle* in September 1983. There were a number of small items about school awards, a fourth-grade school play, an honorable mention in a citywide art show in middle school, art shows and awards in high school . . ."

As she speaks a shiver creeps down my neck and along my backbone. I hold my breath. It's hard to breathe.

Mom doesn't have a clue. "Were the clippings about Mr. Merson's son?" she asks. Her voice is low with concern. "You said that he'd had a son who's no longer living."

Sergeant Balker suddenly speaks, his voice low and quiet. "They're not about Merson's son," he says. "The clippings all have to do with your daughter. The file is labeled 'Kristin Anne Evans.'"

CHAPTER TWO

— // —

There are more questions, and—worst of all—detectives show me photos. My hands shake as I see myself caught in time, totally unaware of a camera. There are pictures of a younger me, taking a bow after a ballet recital, and walking up the steps to someone's front door. I'm carrying a beautifully wrapped birthday present, and my flyaway blond hair is captured in a gigantic white bow. But there are later pictures . . . current pictures. In one photo I'm talking to Lindy, my best friend, while we wait for the school bus. In another I'm shopping in the mall with Mom, and there's a picture of me watering our front lawn in the shade of the elm tree.

The skin on my back prickles. I've been targeted.

I've been spied on. I've been photographed. And I didn't know it was happening.

Sergeant Balker takes one look at me, then turns to Mom and Dad. Maybe he thinks he can spare me some of the horror and outrage I feel if he talks *about* me instead of *to* me. "There's a possibility Kristi was being stalked," he says.

"Stalked?" I'm so shocked I can only stupidly repeat the word. Mom and Dad are too stunned to say anything, but Mom grips my shoulder and hangs on, as if she'll never let me go.

Balker continues. "Did Kristi ever suspect she was being followed? Have there been phone calls? Threats?"

"No!" My voice cracks, but I manage to speak up first. "Nothing like that."

Sergeant Nims breaks in. "Douglas Merson seems to have taken a strong interest in you, Kristin. We need to know why. Do you have any idea?"

Her look is almost accusing, and some of my shock turns to anger. "Why ask me?" I demand. "Why not ask Mr. Merson?"

"I'm asking *you*," she answers.

Sergeant Balker's drawl is reassuring, smoothing Nims's sharp edges. "Merson can't talk to us. Among other things, his jaw was fractured by one of the bullets that hit him, and right now he's full of medicine to kill the pain. The doctors had to do a lot of work to put his jaw back together again."

Mom's sympathy takes over. "The poor man," she murmurs. "Is he going to recover?"

"They think so. Two bullets, but they missed the

brain and the other vital spots. That's what the docs told us."

"Do you have a picture of him?" I ask.

My question startles both detectives. "The crime scene photographs wouldn't be appropriate for you to see," Sergeant Nims tells me.

"That's not what I meant," I tell her. "I mean a snapshot, a posed photo—whatever would have been taken during the last few years. I want to see what he looks like. Maybe I'll recognize his face. Maybe not. But I have to know."

"We have no photographs of Merson," Sergeant Balker answers. "He seems to have been camera shy."

A fresh spout of anger bubbles up inside me. "Then I want to see him," I say. My mother's mouth makes a little circle of surprise, and even Sergeant Nims's eyes widen, but I go on. "I have to see this man who was stalking me, even if he can't talk to us. I need to know what he's like."

Sergeant Nims shakes her head. "From what you've just told us, it doesn't seem likely you were stalked. A stalker usually tries to frighten his victim. That's a major part of his plan. In your case all we have is evidence that Merson was putting together some sort of record or report about you."

"But what about the photographs?"

"He could have hired someone to take those photos."

"Why?"

Frown lines deepen on Dad's forehead, and I'm startled to see that his skin looks gray, as though all

9

the color has been sucked out. "This Merson . . . he's in the hospital. Does that mean Kristi is out of danger?"

"We don't know that Kristi was ever in danger," Balker drawls, the deep slowness of his words giving them a kind of solid comfort.

"Then why—"

"That's the question we're trying to answer," Nims tells Dad.

Mom has been thinking hard. Little wavy lines in her forehead have puckered together between her eyebrows. "What about Mr. Merson's son?" she asks. "How long ago did he die? Losing a son could be . . ." She shudders, takes a deep breath, and goes on. "I mean, did it affect Mr. Merson mentally? Could he have picked a child—any child—as a kind of replacement?"

In the silence that follows we all stare at Mom, but she answers her own question. Her face flushes with embarrassment. "Sorry. I guess that's too far-fetched."

"Anything's possible," Balker says, and he gives Mom a reassuring smile. "That's what Detective Nims and I are here for—to find the answers. We'll check it all out."

"What does Douglas Merson do for a living?" Dad asks. "Perhaps that might give us a clue as to why he has some sort of special interest in Kristi."

A quick glance passes between Nims and Balker before Nims says, "His occupation doesn't seem relevant."

I'm more blunt than Dad. I don't hesitate to ask, "Why don't you want us to know?"

Nims tightens up again, but Balker shrugs and smiles. "Kristi, we're not trying to keep things from you. We don't have the facts ourselves. Merson lives well—*very* well, but we've just begun this investigation. Right now we aren't sure ourselves where the money comes from."

"We're not at liberty to discuss this," Nims says.

Sometimes I watch cop shows on TV, so I've seen the good cop–bad cop routine. I always thought it was something made up for television, but now I know it's for real. And I know Sergeant Balker is a lot easier to talk to than Sergeant Nims. If there really was something about Douglas Merson I wanted to tell them, I'd go to Balker, not Nims. Is that why they're doing this? Or are they acting the way they normally act and I'm only imagining we're in the middle of a planned routine?

"The one who died—what was his name?" I ask the detectives.

Nims raises one eyebrow. "We told you. The victim didn't die, and his name is Douglas Merson."

"Not the victim. The son. What was his son's name?"

"Oh," she says. "The son. Roger. His name was Roger Merson." She studies Mom and Dad. "Does that name mean anything to you?"

"No," Dad says.

All the wavy lines draw together again as Mom shakes her head. "It means nothing at all," she says.

"How old was Roger when he died?" I ask. "Was he a little kid?"

Nims impatiently shoves her pen and pad into her handbag, but Balker says, "He was twenty-one."

He answers the next question as if he knows I'm going to ask it. "Suicide."

He hands each of us one of his business cards and gets to his feet. "If you think of anything you can tell us—" he begins.

But I jump up and face him. "I really do want to see Douglas Merson," I say.

Nims pops up from her chair and straightens her skirt. "I don't think that can be arranged."

"Why not?" I try to pin her down. "In school in American history class I learned that every citizen has a right to face his accuser. This is the same kind of thing, isn't it? I mean, our family is involved with this man, who—for no reason—has kept a secret file—on me. I have a right to see him. I need to find out exactly who he is and if he looks familiar. I'll tell you so it will help your investigation."

"Kristi, dear," Mom says quietly, and puts an arm around my shoulders.

I shrug it off and step forward. "I should have the right," I tell the detective again. "Just because I'm only sixteen, just because you consider me a kid, doesn't mean I can forget about what happened. This man butted into my life. I need to know why. I need to see him."

Nims's face tightens into what is going to become a "no," but Balker steps between us. "We'll ask the docs," he says. "Merson is in intensive care right now, so I doubt if they'd let you in. But when they give the word, I'll be in touch."

He smiles. After a moment I reluctantly smile back. It's easy to see from the crinkle lines around his eyes and the corners of his mouth that Balker

12

smiles a lot. He has a nice face. I like him. I decide I'm going to believe him.

Mom has one more question. "Is any information about our family going to be in the newspaper or on television? Are we going to have to hide Kristi from reporters and photographers?"

"The information about the folder hasn't been released to the media," Nims assures Mom with a hard look.

But Mom isn't satisfied. The look she gives Nims is every bit as steely. "And it won't be?"

"I can't promise anything," Nims says.

Balker steps on Nims's words. "Sooner or later the story is bound to come out. A folder kept on a girl who doesn't even know the man—it's unusual, which means it's what they call newsworthy. But by the time the media hears the story, we hope to find out what the folder is all about so we can wrap up that part of the case. Okay?"

Mom reluctantly nods agreement, but after the detectives leave she gives me a worried look. "Don't be frightened by all this, honey," she says. "You're going to be all right. You'll be safe. The police—"

She breaks off and stares at Dad. "We should have asked about police protection. We can't leave Kristi alone. Somebody should always be with her, even at school. I know this is our busiest season of the year, but we can hire some part-time help for the clerical work—maybe a university student from Rice or the University of Houston—"

Mom is like a wind-up toy with new batteries, ready to go on for hours without stopping, so I grab

13

her shoulders to interrupt her. "Mom, nobody's after me. No stalker. No threats. Some guy has just kept pictures. No one's going to hurt me."

"We don't know that," she says quickly.

"Yes, we do. Douglas Merson is the one who was shot, not me. That shooting has nothing to do with us."

"In a way it does," Dad tells me. "We wouldn't have been aware of that folder if the police hadn't discovered it."

Mom's question comes out like a wail. "Oh, Drew, what does all this mean?"

Dad's answer is little more than a whisper. "I don't know, Callie. Apparently, no one knows."

"Douglas Merson does," I say. "And I'm going to ask him."

"Oh, for goodness' sakes, Kristi, be reasonable," Mom says. "You heard the police tell us that he's in intensive care and can't have visitors." She turns toward the kitchen. "I know. I'll call one of my clients, Edna Grayburn. With her public relations job, she knows something about nearly everyone in Houston. Maybe she can tell us about—"

"But we didn't finish," I complain.

"Finish what?"

"What we were talking about when the detectives came. About my application to that summer art program. It will help if I'm going to major in art in college, and—"

Mom claps her hands over her ears and squeezes her eyes shut. "Oh, please, honey! Not one more word! We've said enough about it already! Pick a career that will support you. Can't you see that

14

those little cartoons you like to draw will never pay the bills?"

"Drawing cartoons is just part of what I do. You know I've even won awards for my watercolors. Ms. Montero is a terrific art teacher. I trust her. And she tells me over and over that I have real artistic talent. She wants me to develop it when I go to college. She says the world would be a happier place if everyone loved their job."

I can hear the hurt in Mom's voice, and I wince, as she says, "Do you care more about what Ms. Montero says than what we tell you? Think about it, Kristi. Ms. Montero isn't going to pay for your college education. Your father and I are going to put out a fortune to get you through college. Shouldn't we have some say in the major you choose?"

Dad steps between Mom and me. "This is no time to talk about college plans. Kristi has almost two years to think about college," he says. "Callie, go ahead and call your client Edna. She may know something about Douglas Merson that will help us figure out what the folder on Kristi is all about."

Mom gives me an agonized look, then leaves for the bedroom phone.

I ask Dad, "When someone's in intensive care, how do you get in to see him?"

"You usually don't, unless you're family," Dad says, and shakes his head.

"I'm just trying to help," I tell him. "And besides, it's like the bear. You know?"

For a moment he looks puzzled. Then his eyes spark, and I can see that he has remembered. He

15

smiles at me. "You mean the nightmare bear," he says.

"That's right. The one that I'd dream about and then wake up crying when I was a little kid. You taught me to face the bear and say, 'I'm not afraid of you,' so he'd go away. And finally he did."

"Mr. Merson's real. He's not a nightmare bear," Dad says.

"But I have to face him, Dad—just like I did with the bear. I have to know what he looks like. And I have to know why he kept a folder of pictures and stuff about me. You understand, don't you?"

Dad nods. "I understand, Kristi. I'm your father. I want to know too. You'll have to be patient. So will I. Ben Taub Hospital has one of the best emergency rooms in Houston, and most gunshot victims are taken there. But Mr. Merson's a wealthy man. When he's able to leave intensive care, he'll probably transfer to a smaller, private hospital. Then Detective Balker can arrange a visit."

"But—"

"You don't have a choice," Dad says firmly.

Oh, yes, I do, I tell myself. This intrusion is something that makes me totally uncomfortable. It's terribly important to me to see Douglas Merson. I am not a baby. Hospital rules or no rules—I must see him as soon as I can, no matter what anyone says.

16

CHAPTER THREE

//

Our Sunday-morning newspaper is still on the kitchen table. The story about the shooting is on the front page of the *Chronicle*, and there's a picture of Merson's house, with crime tape stretched around the trees on the broad front yard. No address. Just the description "posh River Oaks home." But down in the story is the name of the street: Buffalo Bayou Lane. I stare at the photograph until I memorize the look of the house.

It's a large, modernistic, two-story, white brick building with a tile roof, and three rounded steps up to a gigantic front door with a center panel of leaded glass. The house stretches wide wings out among the trees, some of the oaks dripping with strands of gray moss, and there are huge windows everywhere. The house is a light, bright spot in spite of the heavy shade, and the front yard is so beautiful it could only have been planted by a landscape designer.

There are no photographs of Merson with the story, as I thought there surely must be.

Who are you? I silently ask. *Why did you suddenly shove your way into my life? I didn't ask you to.*

I'm scared at what I'm about to do. Maybe Mom's right. Maybe someone besides Merson has been stalking me to take those photos, so I should keep someone by my side and not go out alone. But it can't be Mom. And not Dad. Not with what I plan to do. With them everything is rules, regulations, and order, in tidy, even columns. Sometimes those things come in handy, sometimes I even appreciate them, but right now rules are the last things I need.

I snatch up my purse and car keys. As though it's a good-luck charm, I tuck Detective Balker's card into my bag.

Dad's in the same spot where I left him, sitting motionless, frowning at something invisible. "Could I take your car or Mom's?" I ask him. "Mom's going to be on the phone for hours and hours—maybe days. Edna talks forever, and Mom will want to call Grandma and Aunt Darlene. I want to tell Lindy what happened. I'd rather see her than wait for the phone."

Dad's frown deepens. "We aren't sure who took the photos of you. And your mother suggested asking for police protection. I think maybe you should stay home, or one of us should be with you, Kristi."

"Surely, if I were in danger, the detectives would have said so."

"Maybe you should check your plans with your mother."

"Mom's upset right now. She won't want to be interrupted—especially if Edna is giving her some important information."

I want to win this argument, so I try hard to stay calm and rational and not get all excited and lose my temper. When Mom blows up, she claims it's because teenagers are so exasperating. When I do, she says it's because I'm immature. Sometimes it's a no-win with Mom. Dad's easier to deal with. "I'll be with Lindy," I reassure him. "Nothing's going to happen to me."

Dad thinks about what I've said for a long, miserable moment. Then he nods. "Well, in the days ahead you'll have to go to school, Kristi, and your mother and I will have to go to work. I guess we can't be with you every minute. I think you're correct in saying that the police would have warned us if they felt protection was necessary."

"Are you telling me I can go to Lindy's?" I ask.

Dad flicks one quick, anxious glance in the direction of my mother's voice. Then he says, "Go ahead, honey. Just be watchful. Be extra careful."

"I will, Dad," I tell him. I kiss him on his forehead and leave as quickly and quietly as I can. I'm shaky. My stomach hurts. I'm scared. My fingers tremble as I shove the key into the ignition of Dad's car.

The street is empty. Except for two cars parked

down the street, no one's in sight. As I leave the driveway I carefully watch the parked cars in my rearview mirror. Neither of them starts up. In fact, they're both empty. *Don't think about being followed,* I tell myself. *No one's going to come after you.*

Dad's little four-door, four-cylinder dark blue sedan is quiet and respectable and dull. To get my mind off what I'm doing, I pretend—as I often do—that his car is a low-slung red Lamborghini. In no time I drive the dozen blocks to Lindy's house. I wonder if I ever will be lucky enough to drive an expensive sports car. I like bright splashes of color. It's hard to figure out why both my parents are content to wrap themselves in dark shades of brown, gray, or navy blue.

As I pull into Lindy's driveway, she's out on the lawn in grass-stained shorts, her red hair like fireworks in the strong sunlight. I can see that she's been trying to teach Snickers, her cat, to catch a Frisbee. Snickers, of course, couldn't be more bored and uncooperative. That doesn't seem to bother Lindy, who picks up Snickers, nuzzles the top of her head, and grins into the open driver's window. "What's up, Kristi?" she asks.

"Ask your mom if you can come with me," I tell her.

Lindy pushes her hair from her eyes and takes a step toward her front door. "Where are we going? The mall?"

"Not exactly," I say. "I've got something to—um—show you."

"You're not going to tell me?"

"I will, once we're on our way," I answer.

Lindy shrugs. "Okay. I'll just tell my mom you've got a surprise for me."

I hope the excuse will be enough. There's no way her mom can know we're going to Ben Taub Hospital. She'd call my mom, and my mom would . . . Forget it. I'm not exactly lying. I'm just not telling everything I know. There's a difference.

While I'm waiting for Lindy, I pull out a map book from under the driver's seat and look up the directions to Ben Taub. I've been in the area fairly often. Rice University. Hermann Park. The Museum of Fine Arts. The zoo. And blocks and blocks and blocks of hospitals in a gigantic medical center. I find the Ben Taub area and plan my route. I'm too shaky to drive the freeways, so I'll zigzag from Briar Forest to Westpark, cut over to Kirby and down to Sunset, and take Fannin to MacGregor and the Ben Taub Loop. The map shows a parking garage next to the hospital.

Hurry up, Lindy. Hurry up, hurry up. I drum my fingers on the steering wheel. It's going to take at least forty-five minutes to get there.

The passenger door flies open and Lindy—cleaned up and tidy—shoots in. "What?" she cries as she bangs the door shut. "Tell me. What, what, what?"

I carefully back out of the driveway and head down the street, just in case her mother runs outside to find out more. Again I'm wary about being followed, but there's no sign that anyone's after me.

"I'll tell you," I promise Lindy. "Pay attention, and don't interrupt, no matter what I say. We have to stay cool, because we're going to do something

21

that might be against the rules, and we can't get caught."

"Caught doing what?" Lindy squeaks. Her eyes are huge as she stares at me.

"I'll get to that," I tell her. "Just listen. I'm going to start at the very beginning. Someone's been spying on me, and Lindy . . . I'm scared!"

CHAPTER FOUR

—————— // ——————

When I finish my story, Lindy just stares ahead for a few minutes without speaking. Then she says, "We aren't his relatives. We aren't even his friends. They'll never let us in to see him."

"Not us. Me. I'll go in. You'll stand guard."

I can hear Lindy gulp. "Guard? I won't be any good as a guard. Nurses intimidate me. Did I tell you about when I had my tonsils out and I—"

"Yes. A couple of times," I interrupt. "But no one's going to do anything more than tell you that you don't belong there and you have to leave."

"And you, too."

"I know. But all I need is one minute with Mr. Merson. I just need to see his face. You understand how I feel, don't you?"

Lindy nods. "Sure. I'm curious, too. While you were telling me about him, I was trying to picture what he looked like. How old is he?"

"They didn't say. But he's old enough to have a grown-up son."

"Right. You said his son's name was Roger, and he was twenty-one when he died. How long ago was that?"

"I didn't ask the police."

"I would have," Lindy says. "I should have been there with you." She looks pleased with herself.

"I wish you had been," I tell her. "But at least you're with me now."

"And I'll be at your side right up to the very moment they throw us out of the hospital."

"They won't throw us out."

"Want to bet? People take one look at a couple of teenagers and immediately suspect they're up to no good."

"Not when they're with adults. Then they don't pay any attention to them."

Lindy sighs. "But we won't be with any adults."

"Yes, we will," I tell her. "I've been thinking about it. Ben Taub is a huge, busy community hospital with people going in and out. We'll just watch for someone old enough to be our mother and walk in when she does, trying to look like we're with her."

Traffic grows heavier as people come out of late church services and head for favorite restaurants or home. When we reach the Ben Taub parking garage we have to get into a slow-moving line.

"It must be visiting hours," Lindy says.

24

"Good. It will make our visit even easier."

Luckily, on the third floor a driver pulls out of a visitor's space, and I drive in. Lindy and I travel down the elevator and across an open walkway to the hospital entrance.

"Visiting a patient?" a guard at the lobby door asks me.

I answer, "Yes," and he points to a glassed-in walkway with a metal detector, like those in an airport.

"You gotta go through there," he says.

Lindy and I put our bags on the belt to be run through the X rays, and we walk through the metal detector without setting anything off. The woman behind me places on the belt a large, wrapped gift box. It disappears into the X-ray machine.

"Why do they do this?" Lindy whispers to me.

I look at her without answering. Some of the people brought here for care are on the wrong side of the law. Some people are crazy. Lindy knows that. It's just not something I want to think about.

Ben Taub is a bright, clean hospital with plenty of directional signs. We spot the ICU info, make a turn past the gift shop to the nearest elevators, and go to the fourth floor, to the intensive care unit.

A sign over a door says WAITING ROOM, so Lindy and I slip inside. A few of the people seated on the molded plastic chairs look up at us, but their eyes are dulled with worry, so their curiosity doesn't last long. There are two empty chairs next to an untidy woman who slumps in her seat. Lindy and I quietly sit down while I try to decide what to do next.

Visiting hours for intensive care patients are

posted. Three times a day. One of the times is one to one-thirty. I look at my watch. I feel lucky. It's five after one. I don't have much time.

A man lumbers through the door and drops into a chair next to the woman seated beside me. "She's doing okay," he says in an exhausted voice. "She wants to see you."

The woman stiffens. "Do I have to?"

The man lowers his voice. "She's always been good to you," he says. "Go see her. Let her talk. It's the least you can do."

The woman turns her head away from him and gives a grunt of disapproval, but she hoists herself out of her chair and waddles toward the door.

"Come on," I whisper to Lindy.

We follow the woman around the corner to a station where a nurse is seated at a desk. A stocky woman in a security uniform stands next to her. They take a good look at the woman, and the nurse at the desk asks, "Name of patient?"

"Fritz. Imogene Fritz," the woman mumbles.

The nurse nods. "You'll go through two automatic doors. Press the square buttons on the wall at the right of the doors. They'll open the doors for you."

"Ask the nurse a question," I whisper to Lindy. "Block her view."

As Lindy leans across the desk, I join the woman, as though I'm her daughter, and pass through the electronic doors to the intensive care unit.

Another nurse looks at us both. "Wash your hands before visiting the patient," she says. "And when you leave, wash your hands again."

26

I wash and dry my hands at the sink she points to, then step out of her sight. There are beds in two rows along the outside walls. Around each of them is equipment, from IV holders to monitor screens. They look familiar since I sometimes watch the hospital shows on TV.

Down the center is an array of cabinets, sinks, and everything else the nurses need to work with. I'm thankful for this barrier, which hides me from the nurse on duty.

Quickly I eye the charts at the foot of the beds where there are no visitors. On my third try, down near the end of the room, I find the name Douglas Merson.

It's hard to breathe. I'm dizzy, and I hope I won't pass out. I take small, shallow breaths as I scoot around the bed and stand at the side where I can look down on Merson's face.

As I grip the guardrail on the bed, I whimper. I don't mean to react, but I can't help it. I see only the small part of his face that isn't swathed in bandages or hooked up to tubes. Merson's eyes and forehead are exposed and there's a slit where his mouth should be, but his eyes are closed. Has he heard me? Does he know I'm here?

"Who are you?" I whisper.

He doesn't respond. Just like the other patients, he's attached to electric monitors and IV drips. His monitor makes a steady green line of jumps and wiggles and it beeps in rhythm, which must mean that his heart is beating the way it's supposed to.

I take a long, deep breath and try to think of Plan B. Only there is no Plan B. I knew Merson was

27

hurt. I should have realized that his face would be bandaged. I don't think things through, as Mom sometimes reminds me.

I take a closer look at Mr. Merson. His light blond hair is streaked with gray. It probably thinned as he grew older, but he hasn't begun to go bald. His shoulders are definitely broad, he's tall, and I guess—from the way the sheet mounds over his body—that he isn't thin, but he isn't fat, either. I imagine he takes pretty good care of himself.

I remember reading once that sometimes people in a coma can hear when music is played or they're spoken to. I don't know if Mr. Merson is in a coma, or if he's just out of it because he's been given pain pills. But on the chance he can hear me I lean forward, resting my arms on the guardrail.

"I'm Kristi Evans," I say quietly. "I came to see you because the police told us that you kept a folder with information about me in it. They showed me some of the photographs."

I don't know why, but, standing beside his bed, I'm not afraid of Douglas Merson any longer. My curiosity and fear have turned to pity. This man in the intensive care unit lies helpless. "I'm sorry you were shot," I tell him. "But you survived, so when you get a little better you can tell the police who did it. And you can tell me—will you please, please tell me?—why you've saved things about me ever since I was a baby. I have to know."

Maybe, at the back of my mind, I've been hoping for a sign like a wiggle of his fingers or flutter of his eyelids, so I'll know he heard me. But his eyes don't

28

open, and the beeping machine keeps up its steady rhythm.

Suddenly a nurse appears beside me. "Are you a family member?" she asks.

I sorrowfully look away from Mr. Merson and shake my head. "I'm a friend. I heard he was shot in the jaw, but his nose is bandaged too. What happened to his face?"

"Broken nose, skin abrasions. He'll be eating all his meals through a straw for a while." She smiles at me. "Better leave now and let him sleep."

"I'll come back, Mr. Merson," I tell him. "When you can have visitors, I'll come and see you."

He gently breathes in and out. He doesn't show that he hears me.

The nurse leads me out to the waiting room. I motion to Lindy, and we walk to the elevators. We soon find ourselves back in the parking garage, headed for Dad's car.

The moment we're seated, Lindy asks, "Okay, tell me. What does he look like? Have you seen him before?"

I sigh. "Most of his face was covered with bandages." As I drive out of the parking garage I add, "He didn't look like a monster, Lindy. He looked kind of sad, and pitiful, and old. He's probably almost as old as Grandma."

As we cross Main and head for Kirby, I look at my watch. "We're awfully close to the Museum of Fine Arts. Want to stop in for a little while?"

Lindy laughs. "Your home away from home? Not today."

29

Even with everything that's happened, visiting the museum seems sane to me.

"They're showing an exhibition of early sketches by Picasso. Ms. Montero said my style reminds her a little bit of his during his early period. I've been wanting my parents to go with me, but with everyone needing their income tax figured out, Mom and Dad have been too busy."

Lindy laughs. "Your parents think in terms of accounting stuff, and you're so different. I'm just like my mom. Even in looks," she says, pointing to her wild hair.

"Maybe I'm a changeling," I tell her. "I'm a true fairy child, given to hardworking accountants to raise. Someday I'll break out of the mold and turn into a famous artist, and then everyone will know. And they'll be sorry they told me I'd waste time and money getting a degree in art."

Lindy puts a hand on my arm. "Hey, don't look so serious, Kristi," she says. "You've told me that your grandmother says you take after her oldest brother, Elton. Maybe Elton drew like Picasso too."

"I don't know," I answer. "Grandma said Elton was too busy running his farm up in Oklahoma to do much with his art. In our family I seem to be one of a kind."

Lindy suddenly says, "What are you looking for? You're jumpy, and you keep staring into your rearview mirror. You think we're being followed, don't you?"

"I know we're not," I tell her. "I'm just—oh, I don't know. My mind is wandering and now what the detectives told us shook me up."

30

"Are you too nervous to drive home through River Oaks, instead of down Westpark?" Lindy asks. "Maybe we can see the house where Douglas Merson lives. Want to?"

"Yes," I answer quickly, surprised at my eagerness. I can feel the pressure of excitement in my chest. I wonder why I didn't think of this myself.

"Can you find the house?" Lindy asks. "Do you have Douglas Merson's address?"

"I know what it looks like, from the newspaper photo, and that it's on a street called Buffalo Bayou Lane." I pull up to a stoplight at Kirby and Alabama and tug the map book out from under the seat. As I hand it to Lindy I ask, "Look it up for me, will you? You can give me directions."

In just a few minutes Lindy says, "We're on Kirby, so when we get to Inwood, turn left. Keep going a little way past River Oaks Boulevard. Buffalo Bayou Lane comes in on the right and winds to the north. Hey! It's right next to the bayou itself."

"Which is why, boys and girls, the street's named Buffalo Bayou Lane. Surprise!" I say.

"Very funny," Lindy answers. "I don't think I'd want to live next to one of the bayous. All the bayous in Houston are muddy and yucky and full of snakes." She scratches her chin. "My dad says property along the bayous is more valuable because the bayous offer more privacy. But I think there's another reason—guard snakes, to keep burglars from sneaking up on back doors."

"Guard snakes?" I laugh. "Now I've heard everything."

"I'm serious," Lindy says. "If you were a burglar,

31

would you want to go squishing through a bayou with poisonous snakes in it?"

"What about hanging boa constrictors in the trees?"

"Sure. They could be imported."

Lindy keeps going on about guard snakes, and soon we're both laughing. I know that Lindy's trying to keep me from worrying about what's happened. Mom and Dad think of Lindy as an airhead because she had to be tutored through algebra II, but I know she's sharp where it really counts.

It doesn't take long to get to Buffalo Bayou Lane. I turn right and follow the narrow road that winds among the trees. The homes are far apart and set back from the street. We pass a French chateau, a huge stone house that looks like an English castle, and a plantation home right out of a *Gone With the Wind* movie set. At the curve, where Buffalo Bayou makes a sharp bend, we suddenly come upon Douglas Merson's house—very modern and stark white.

Lindy sucks in her breath. "Wow!" she says. "That's where he lives? Really?"

"Really," I answer. The yellow strips of crime tape have been taken away. Nothing should spoil the beauty of this setting.

But something did spoil it. Attempted murder.

Without planning to, I find myself steering the car up the long drive toward the house.

"Hey!" Lindy whispers, and she stiffens. "What are you doing?"

"Somebody must be inside," I tell her. "It's a big house. I'm sure Mr. Merson doesn't live there alone."

"But if his wife comes to the door, what will you say?"

"They said he isn't married. Whoever answers the door will probably be someone who works for him."

"Wow!" Lindy says again. "A butler, maybe? Like in British films? I've never seen a real live butler."

I park next to the steps to the front door and slowly get out of the car. I've made a mistake. I should jump back in the car and quickly drive away. But Lindy is following my example. She's out of the car, ready for what I'm going to do next.

I can't run. I have to finish what I started. I get the weird feeling that someone inside the house is watching me.

Gulping down my fear, I take one step at a time, climb the brick steps, and ring the doorbell.

I don't have time to catch my breath before the door opens wide. I was right. Someone was there.

CHAPTER FIVE

———— // ————

The man who stands in the doorway reminds me of the background figures in some of the Dutch masters' paintings—solid, solemn, and totally interchangeable. Average face, average brown hair, average height—about five ten. He's wearing a tan shirt and slacks that seem designed to make him look unimportant. "What can I do for you?" he asks, and even his voice is forgettable.

I wish I'd planned something intelligent to say. "This is my friend Lindy Baker, and my name is Kristi Evans," I announce. I wait for his reaction. If he lives here—or even just works here—he probably knows about Mr. Merson's folder about me, doesn't he?

His eyes don't flicker. His eyebrows don't twitch. His expression doesn't change. He looks as if he's never heard of me.

"Kristi Evans," I repeat.

"What can I do for you, Ms. Evans?" he asks.

"You can tell me something about Mr. Douglas Merson," I say.

"About his medical condition?" I catch a note of surprise. "I'm sorry," he says firmly. "There is nothing I can tell you." The door begins to close.

"Wait! Please wait!" I call. I have no idea what to say. I just blurt out, "The police have been to see me and my parents. Two detectives told us that Mr. Merson has kept a folder about me, but I've never even met Mr. Merson. I need to know who he is and *why* he has a folder about me!"

"I know nothing about—" the man begins. But he breaks off, looking at a car that has shot into the driveway.

With a screech of brakes a gold Infiniti comes to a stop just behind Dad's car. The door flies open, and a woman slides out.

I see her blue silk suit, which is really expensive, and her dark, sleek haircut, which makes her look as if she stepped out of a fashion magazine. Gold shines at her ears, throat, and wrist; rings on both hands flash in the sunlight.

At first I think she's in her late twenties or early thirties, but as she strides toward us I can see there's a thick layer of makeup over a face that's probably in Mom's age group. She's tall and slender and looks good, though.

35

She throws Lindy and me a quick glance, then ignores us. Probably thinks we're selling raffle tickets door-to-door for our school. "Frederick!" she calls. "I'm glad you're here! I just heard about poor, dear Douglas, and I'm devastated."

"Good afternoon, Ms. Chase," Frederick says. I notice he keeps a firm grip on the door.

"Tell me what happened to Douglas," Ms. Chase cries. Her voice stretches higher and tighter, and she speaks so fast that her words stumble into each other. "Of course, I know you weren't here, since Saturdays are your days off, but you can tell me what the police told you. If only I'd been on hand. I was out of town—Austin, a new gallery opening. Ilsa's gallery. She's not exactly a friend, but I felt I had to be there. She used to work with me."

Ms. Chase gulps in a breath and rushes on. "You know how boring some of those openings can be, and this one was. I had a raging headache from the champagne—not the best quality, which I should have expected—and the Four Seasons is comfortable—the only place I ever stay in Austin—so I didn't drive back to Houston until this afternoon. When I heard the news on my car radio, I simply came apart. Imagine Douglas being shot in the head. I can't believe he's still alive!" Her words run down long enough for her mind to take over. "He *is* going to survive, isn't he?"

"You'll have to ask his doctors," Frederick answers.

Ms. Chase doesn't give up easily. She runs up the steps, elbowing me aside, and leans one hand against the massive door. If Frederick decides to close it, I think he's going to have a shoving match on his hands, and Ms. Chase looks strong enough to win. I bet she works out regularly. "The staff at the hospital won't tell me anything," she says. "I need to talk to Douglas's personal physician. Who is he?"

"I'm not at liberty to give out personal information about Mr. Merson," Frederick answers.

Ms. Chase reminds me of a rubber band tightly stretched. I expect her to let go and shoot off at any minute, but she surprises me. She gives herself a little shake, as though she's putting all the pieces back together, and smiles at Frederick. "This is all terribly upsetting to you, isn't it?" she asks him. "You've worked for Douglas ten . . . twelve . . . how many years? And I'm sure you count him as a good friend, as well as an employer." She lets out a long, painful sigh. "All of us share the same grief, Frederick."

"Thank you, Ms. Chase," Frederick says quietly.

She waits, as though she's expecting him to say something else, but he stands motionless. I'm beginning to think Frederick doesn't give information—even an opinion—to anyone. But I don't leave. Ms. Chase obviously talks as if we don't count. I'm curious to hear if she can get anything out of him.

She goes on, "Now, Frederick, I'm going to ask you to do something. It's not for me. Oh no, it's definitely not a favor for me. It's for poor, dear Douglas."

She pauses and dramatically sighs again. I'm totally caught up in this conversation, hoping for some clue.

"Douglas has two paintings for the gallery," Ms. Chase tells Frederick. "I was supposed to pick them up when I returned from Austin, so I'm sure they're wrapped and ready. May I have them, please?"

I'm positive Frederick will say he doesn't know anything about them, so I'm surprised when he holds the door open wide and steps aside so that Ms. Chase can enter. She trots across the hall and up the broad stairway.

I suck in my breath as I'm treated to a view of an entry hall right out of the pages of a designer magazine. My eyes survey the place quickly. The room is round, with a staircase that curves down the right side, and it's light and bright with sunlight streaming through the broad front windows. A table with a crystal vase of white gladioli stands at the center of the room, but what catches my eye and holds it is on the wall facing the door. A canvas is covered with vertical splashes of reds, oranges, yellows, blues, and greens that shimmer like a stained-glass window. At the top of the painting a woman's face peers down through the blinding strips of color.

"I think of her as the heart and soul of the painting," Ms. Montero told our art class as she showed us a slide of this painting. I've forgotten the name of the painting, but I can remember the name of the artist—Frank Kupka. I also remember that the painting is supposed to be hanging in New York's Museum of Modern Art.

Puzzled, I actually step forward to see better. It is

not a print, and it's not a lithograph. I can see the strong brush strokes in the oil paint.

Suddenly Frederick steps in front of me, blocking my view. As Frederick moves forward, I stumble back, my face burning with embarrassment. I've entered this house without being invited, and now I'm being forced to leave. When I reach the front steps I stammer, "I—I'm sorry. The painting . . . it's so beautiful . . . I had to get a closer look . . . I wasn't thinking."

Frederick gives a stiff nod, then silently closes the big door.

Lindy waits on the drive. She looks a little scared. "What were you doing?" she asks me as I join her.

"There's a painting in the entry hall. I mean a real painting. The real thing, Lindy. It's gorgeous."

Lindy gives me an odd look. "What's so exciting about somebody having a painting in his house? Lots of people do."

"Not this painting. This is a museum piece. I saw it on a slide in Ms. Montero's class. But she said it was hanging in the Museum of Modern Art in New York."

Lindy climbs into the passenger seat of the car and fastens her seat belt. "Calm down," she tells me. "Douglas Merson obviously has a lot of money. He probably got the artist to paint another, just like the one in the museum."

"No way," I insist. "The artist who painted it died around the late fifties—1957, I think Ms. Montero said."

As I begin to follow the curve of the drive, I

39

glance back at the house. There's a shadow in one of the entry hall windows. Frederick. He's standing there watching. I shiver.

I turn onto Buffalo Bayou Lane, looking for a cross street that will cut through to San Felipe, and think out loud. "Ms. Montero told us that lots of artists have made copies of their own work, like Van Gogh, who copied his painting of sunflowers for his friend Paul Gauguin. And Stuart, who painted more than seventy-five copies of his famous 'Athenaeum Head' painting of George Washington to get out of debt.

"Sometimes artists wanted to save what they'd done, but thought of ways of making their paintings better by changing just one little thing, so they'd paint practically the same scene. And some of the artists way back when, like Rembrandt, assigned students and assistants to copy their work. Ms. Montero told us that Rembrandt even signed some of their paintings with his own name. Maybe this is one of those almost-alike paintings."

"Ask Ms. Montero," Lindy answers. I can hear the boredom in her voice. She doesn't share my interest in art, and if I talk about it too long she clicks a switch in her brain and tunes me out. I can't get that fantastic painting with its explosion of color out of my mind, but to please Lindy I search for something else to talk about.

Lindy suddenly stares at me, then turns and glances out the back window of the car. "Nobody's following us," she says.

"What?"

"You keep looking in the rearview mirror every few seconds, Kristi, like you think someone's going to look back. If you weren't already jumpy enough to drive into a tree, I'd be tempted to yell, 'Boo!' " She shakes her head. "You know for a fact that Mr. Merson's in the hospital. You saw him there."

"I know. But now that we've seen how Mr. Merson lives and how rich he must be, I can't imagine that he's the one who followed me or took photos of me. It would be more realistic if he hired someone to do it."

"Like Frederick?"

I shiver again. "I don't know."

"He's creepy enough," Lindy says. "I wonder if he feels anything."

I suddenly make a right turn off San Felipe into a quiet side street and pull the car to a stop at the curb.

"Now what?" Lindy asks.

"We asked the wrong person," I tell her.

"Don't say *we. You* did the asking. I didn't ask anybody anything."

"You know what I mean. Look. We found out that Frederick works for Mr. Merson and he's loyal. He made it clear he wouldn't talk about Mr. Merson or anything connected with him. But other people wouldn't feel so loyal. Like neighbors. Or even that Ms. Chase."

Lindy's eyes are wide with surprise. "I don't think any of them would know about the folder."

"I'm not talking about the folder. I'm talking about Douglas Merson. The people who lived next

41

to him would know what he was like. And Ms. Chase said she was a friend. We could find out more about Mr. Merson through them."

"I don't think so," Lindy says. "To begin with, we don't know Ms. Chase's first name. And she looks like the kind of person who'd have an unlisted phone number. How are we going to find her?"

"Easy. She came to pick up two paintings and she talked about a friend who used to work with her and now has her own art gallery. And she said she'd come *back* from Austin, so that means her home is in the Houston area. We can find her by calling the art galleries."

"She'll ignore us again."

"Maybe not. She had her mind set on convincing Frederick to give her the paintings. We weren't of any use to her."

"We still won't be."

I grin at Lindy. "Why don't we find out?"

We cruise back to Buffalo Bayou Lane. Ms. Chase's car is no longer parked in front of the Merson house.

The front windows of the house are as blank as closed eyes, not giving even a hint that behind them hangs one of the most exciting paintings I've ever seen.

The homes on either side of the Merson house snuggle back among the trees like recluses who want to be left alone. Two dark sedans are parked down the street, but not a person is in sight.

Lindy gives an exaggerated sigh and asks, "You're not going to ring doorbells, are you?"

"Good idea," I tell her.

"Kristi! You don't mean it! The people who live in this part of River Oaks don't want to talk to people like us. And listen, it's getting late."

"I'll be quick. And what's wrong with us?"

"You know what I mean. Even if you do get someone to come to the door, it will probably be a maid or a butler." She pauses and adds, "Or someone like Frederick."

But I've come this far, and I know I've only just begun what might be a difficult search for the truth. What does Douglas Merson have to do with me? I have to find out.

As I turn into the long drive that leads to the Louisiana-plantation-style mansion next to Mr. Merson's property, Lindy groans and slumps down in her seat. "I never saw you before in my life," she says. "I'm not going to get out of this car."

"You don't need to," I answer as I park the car. I'd feel a little braver if Lindy stood near me on the veranda, with its gleaming white columns, but this is something I can do without any help.

I hear the doorbell echo through the house, then the click of footsteps. The door swings open, and a short, plump woman dressed in a white uniform smiles up at me. "Yes?" she asks.

I wish I'd planned what to say, but I haven't, so I blurt out, "I'm wondering if you can tell me something about Mr. Merson, who lives next door."

The woman gives me a puzzled look. "You're too young to be a reporter or with the police. Why do you want to know about the shooting?"

"I'm not asking about the shooting," I explain. "I'm asking about Mr. Merson. I want to find out as much as I can about him."

Shaking her head, the woman says, "Mrs. Carmody is in England. She'll return in three weeks. You can come back then." The woman steps away, as if she's going to shut the door.

I let out a groan. I can't help it. I find myself saying, "I have to find out who Douglas Merson is because it has something to do with my family," in my best sweet help-me voice.

The woman's eyes gleam, and the tip of her tongue sweeps one corner of her mouth, as if she's tasting something delicious. She moves closer. "All I know is what I see," she says. She half turns and flicks a glance toward the back of the house. "And what we in the kitchen . . . heard the Carmodys say about him."

I nod. "I understand."

"He comes and goes a lot. Trips to Europe mostly."

I think about the paintings Ms. Chase came to pick up. "Maybe he's an importer," I suggest.

The woman raises one eyebrow, as if that's the last thing she'd consider. "When he's home he gives parties," she tells me. "Lots of expensive cars and people with money, but nobody the Carmodys know. That houseman named Frederick who works there knows what's going on, but he keeps mostly to himself."

"What do you mean, 'what's going on'?" I ask.

She shrugs. "None of us are sure. We're just guessing. You didn't hear it from me."

44

I don't say anything. I just nod again. She's wound up now. She won't need much encouragement to keep talking.

She tilts her head to one side and lowers her voice to a whisper. "When Mr. Merson's in Houston he doesn't go to an office. He doesn't seem to have a job, yet he's got a lot of money. Drives a Rolls and a Ferrari, and I heard tell that his clothes are all custom-made in Italy. You know what that adds up to, don't you?"

I shake my head. "No. I honestly don't know what you mean."

"Drugs," she whispers. "What else?"

"Drugs?" I can only stare stupidly.

"I don't know how you and your family got mixed up with a man like that, but I think you should stay clear of him," she finishes. Her interest in me has vanished, and she studies me as though she wonders if I'm involved in selling drugs too.

"Thank you," I manage to say before she shuts the door. But I wish she hadn't told me. I wish I hadn't asked. Drugs? Merson's a drug dealer?

As I climb into the car I tell Lindy about the conversation, and she reacts with a gasp.

"Let's go home," she says, "and forget all about Douglas Merson. The police are going to take care of things, and they're going to take care of you, Kristi. Snooping around about a drug dealer could be dangerous. Stop asking questions. Give it up."

I don't argue. At the moment I'm ready to forget I ever heard of Douglas Merson.

But as I pull into Buffalo Bayou Lane, one of the black sedans, parked at a curb a half block away, starts up. It stays behind me as I cut down to San Felipe and turn west. The car doesn't pull up close enough so that I can see the driver or anyone else who might be in the car.

It follows me all the way to Lindy's house.

CHAPTER SIX

I drop Lindy off, and the car behind me pulls to the curb a good half block away. Lindy hasn't noticed. She's started comparing the super deli sandwiches at eatZi's and Guggenheim's, and she's so carried away by the vision and anticipation, she hasn't noticed that I've been checking the rearview mirror.

"See you at school tomorrow," she says, and opens her car door. Then she stops and rests a hand on my arm. "Don't worry about Mr. Merson and that folder, Kristi. There has to be a good reason for it, and whatever it is, the police will find out. Let them take care of it. Okay?"

"Okay," I tell her, although I have no intention of following her advice. "See you tomorrow."

I wait until she opens her front door and waves before I head toward home.

The car is still there. It's not far behind me. The stalker is good. I'd never have noticed him if I hadn't been afraid of being shadowed and been especially aware of anything that seemed different.

I know one way to find out who he is . . . if I'm lucky. Near my street is a short cul-de-sac. Without signaling, I turn into it. My stalker is intent on following me, so he turns into the street too, before he can think about what I'm doing. I speed up, swoop around the curve at the end of the street, and drive back, facing him.

He shoots into a driveway, disappearing toward the back of the house, but he's not fast enough. I get a good look at the make of his car and his license plate and memorize the numbers and letters.

He doesn't follow me the rest of the way to my house. He doesn't have to. I think about the photographs taken of me on our front lawn. He knows where I live.

I call a quick hello to my parents, who are both working with tax forms on the computers in the backup office they keep at home.

"Hello, honey," Mom calls. She leaves her work and comes to greet me. Her hug is tight, and I feel a pang of guilt as I realize that she has worried about me. I steel myself to explain what I did, but she doesn't ask. "I know you had to see Lindy," she says quietly. "It's all right, Kristi."

I give Mom an extra hug. Sometimes we don't need to say the words to know how much we're loved.

She smiles at me and says, "I'll finish this form within half an hour . . . or thereabouts."

I laugh as she leaves. I've known those "thereabouts" to stretch over a long period. I wonder what Mom has learned from her client Edna. I'll ask later. There's something I have to do first.

I find Detective Jerry Balker's business card in my wallet and use the extension phone in my bedroom to call his number.

"Homicide. Al Wilson," a deep voice answers.

"May I please speak to Sergeant Balker?" I ask.

"Jerry's not here right now. Do you want to leave a message for him?"

I could ask for Sergeant Nims. No. It takes only a split second to decide. "Yes, I'll leave a message. Thanks." I tell him my name and about being followed and give him the license plate number. "When will Sergeant Balker be back?" I ask.

"I'm not sure," he says. "I'll give him the message."

I start to ask something else, but he's already hung up the phone.

———— // ————

On Sunday evenings we have what Mom calls a "pickup supper." Tonight there are slices of ham and "lite" Swiss cheese, sliced tomatoes and fat dill pickles, and quart cartons of potato salad and coleslaw. Mom and Dad will take the leftovers to work tomorrow for lunch. At dinnertime we relax and talk as much as eat.

But tonight, while we eat, there are no corny

jokes from Dad. Mom tells us that her client Edna knew about Douglas Merson. He is a very wealthy man who travels a lot, mostly to Europe. His wealthy friends fly into Houston in their private jets for his parties. I can tell from Mom's tone of voice that Edna was suitably impressed.

Hoping with all my heart that Edna knew all the answers, I ask Mom, "What does Mr. Merson do for a living?"

"Edna thinks he's in financial investments."

I sag with relief. "Oh. Then he's a broker."

"No," Mom answers. "Edna said he's probably living on the profits from investments he's made, because he doesn't seem to have or need a regular job." I can hear the echo of Edna's attitude in Mom's voice again.

Dad looks up from his plate. He brushes a thin wisp of dark hair from his forehead. "From what she said about the amount of travel he does, they'd have to have been darned good investments."

My fingers feel numb and clumsy, and I drop my fork. Carrying it to the sink and getting a clean one gives me time to get my feelings under control. Should I tell Mom and Dad about the suspicions of Mrs. Carmody's maid? No. They're worried enough already. If they think a drug dealer has an interest in their daughter they'll be terrified.

I realize that Mom has stopped eating and is taking a good, hard look at me. She suddenly asks, "Kristi, you've got something on your mind. What is it?"

I stammer the first thing that comes to the sur-

face, surprising myself. Maybe it's been lurking in my brain from the beginning, hoping I'd discover it. "The police said that Mr. Merson was robbed of his watch, so they're thinking this was a random robbery that turned into attempted murder."

Dad has put down his fork, and he's studying me too. I take a deep breath to steady myself and let the rest of the thought pour out. "But I was wondering, why didn't the robber go into the house? Mr. Merson has—I mean, since he's so rich, he *must* have—a lot of valuable things in his house. He was home alone, and the door was open. All the thief had to do was run inside, grab what he could, and get away fast. But he didn't. Why not?"

Mom sighs. "Honey, how can any of us know what a criminal is thinking? Please don't dwell on the crime. It's depressing."

"I can't help wondering."

Mom reaches out and pats my shoulder. "Sometimes I worry that you're too quick to let your imagination take over. Please, please, stop thinking about that crime. Fill your mind with something pleasant. Will you?"

Both Mom and Dad are looking at me with such pleading in their eyes that I nod. "I'll try," I tell them.

Dad begins talking to Mom about investments in relation to taxes. I tune out. I made a promise, so I'll try to keep it. I stop thinking about the robbery and shooting and think instead about the black Ford sedan that followed me home. I tried to get a look at the driver, but I couldn't. There was a glare of sunlight on the windows, and I could make out only one shadowlike blur inside the car. One driver and no passengers. For some reason I got the impression that the driver was a man.

I don't know why I was being followed. The idea terrifies me.

"Have you got all your homework done, Kristi?" Mom asks. She opens the refrigerator door and puts the cartons of leftover salad inside.

I awake to reality and see that I'm clearing the plates from the table. Have I eaten? I must have. "Uh—homework?" I answer. "Sure. I've finished it." I take a deep breath, grip the edge of the counter for support, and say, "Mom, about that application for the summer art program Ms. Montero gave me for you and Dad to sign—"

"Oh, honey, I don't want to get into that again," Mom says.

"But I need to—"

"That art school is expensive. I wouldn't mind the expense if it would lead you into something practical. But it will just make you more sure of your crazy idea that you want to major in art in college. When you go to college you'll need to major in a subject that will put you into a job with a good salary. Like business, or accounting. I don't understand why you can't take a fair look at accounting. Didn't you understand anything your father and I tried to explain to you?"

Mom's eyes are tired, and her face sags with exhaustion. I know that the news we got about Mr. Merson's folder frightened her, and she's worried about me. I shouldn't have brought up the application again. I realize that. For once, I don't argue. I gulp down the lump of disappointment that tightens my throat and turn back to the sink, scraping the plates and putting them into the dishwasher.

Into my mind comes the picture of Mr. Merson, his head wrapped in bandages, his eyes closed and still. Mom and Dad will be mad at me if they learn I went to see him. But I need to know. *Who are you?* I silently ask, even though no one can answer.

———//———

I have art appreciation class first period, which is the perfect time for it. In the early morning my mind is open, clear, and fresh. It's not cluttered with math problems, and history dates, and gossip, and even zapping thoughts about Jonathan Stockton, who is a really terrific guy in my art class and who so far has paid almost no attention to me.

Ms. Montero takes roll. Then she asks, "How many of you noticed the item in the *Chronicle* this morning about the painting, worth over a million dollars, that was stolen from the Louvre Museum in Paris?"

Only two hands go up. Neither of them are mine. The only way I'd have time to read the newspaper before school is if I got up half an hour early. There's no way I'm going to do that.

"How could someone steal a valuable painting from a big museum like the Louvre?" someone asks. "They have guards and security, don't they?"

"Apparently not enough," Ms. Montero tells us. "Theft is a huge problem at every museum. Even with electronic alarms and armed guards, thieves consistently manage to make away with priceless pieces of art."

Jonathan speaks up. "I don't get it. What kind of market is there for stolen museum art? It's so high profile everyone would recognize it and know where it had come from. The thieves would be arrested if they tried to sell it, wouldn't they?"

Jonathan's voice is low and smooth and is just right for him because he's tall and slender and moves quietly. I've drawn sketches of Jonathan, which he doesn't know about. Even if he someday asks me out . . . even if he someday falls madly in love with me . . . I'll never show him the sketches. They're a secret part of my life where no one else is allowed to go.

"That's a good question, Jonathan," Ms. Montero says. "Unfortunately, there's a large market for expensive masters made up of certain unscrupulous private collectors. Some art thefts, in which a collector wants a particular painting, are even committed on order."

Beth Smith gasps. "You mean a painting that hangs in a museum for hundreds of thousands of people to see and enjoy can end up in someone's house, hidden away?"

Ms. Montero nods.

Andy Wright screws up his face as he thinks. "With so many people watching, I can't see how anyone can steal a painting from a museum."

Ms. Montero sits on the edge of her desk, leaning forward. "According to the newspaper story, the painting came from a room that doesn't have television surveillance. The thief knew that the painting wasn't monitored. Apparently no one else was in the room when he removed the canvas on its stretchers from the back, leaving the frame and glass behind. The same thing happened in the Louvre on a busy Sunday in May 1998. With over thirty thousand people visiting the museum that day, a nineteenth-century landscape by Camille Corot, *The Sevres Road*, was taken in that very same way."

"And nobody saw?"

"Nobody saw." She shakes her head. "Let me tell you about another theft that took place at the Louvre back in 1911. Leonardo da Vinci's *Mona Lisa* was stolen."

Some of the kids gasp, and I say, "But they got it back, didn't they? It's hanging there now."

Ms. Montero smiles. "I'll tell you what happened. A group of art forgers found six American collectors who had no ethics or principles. They told each of them, individually, that they were going to steal the *Mona Lisa* and offered it for three hundred thousand dollars, which was a great deal of money at that time."

"It's a great deal of money right now," Jonathan says under his breath.

I grin to let him know I enjoyed his joke, but he doesn't look in my direction.

"The forgers made six copies of the *Mona Lisa*," Ms. Montero says. "Then they—"

"How?" Beth asks. "How did they copy it?"

"At that time painters were allowed to set up their easels right in the museum so they could work. Many artists learn by copying the masters. This method of study has been practiced for centuries." She pauses, then explains, "Artists are still allowed to copy paintings in museums. However, because of so much forgery in the art field, most museums in Europe no longer allow artists to make copies the same size as the original."

"Do they have that rule in the United States?" Beth interrupts.

"I'm afraid not," Ms. Montero says.

I speak up. "But people could recognize a forgery, couldn't they? New canvas and paint. You told us once that some paints weren't in existence until the mid-eighteen hundreds, like zinc white. Before that time, they used lead white."

"That's correct," Ms. Montero answers. "Tests can be made of the paint. But many forgers buy old paintings just to get the canvases and stretchers. They remove the paintings or paint over them."

She pauses. When no one asks another question, she says, "Now, to go on with my story . . . a thief named Vincenzo Peruggia and two of his associates entered the Louvre on a busy Sunday afternoon and hid in a storage closet.

"The museum was closed for cleaning on Mondays, so the next morning they dressed in workmen's clothes and joined the other workers. On Mondays paintings were occasionally photographed in a special room of the museum, so no one questioned the thieves when they wrapped the painting

56

in a cloth and took it out of the room. They left by a side door that was unguarded, and the theft wasn't discovered until the next day. The six forged paintings had already gone through U.S. customs, and they were soon delivered and paid for. Each of the collectors thought he had received the original *Mona Lisa*."

"What happened to the real *Mona Lisa?*" someone asks.

"Two years later it was recovered when Vincenzo Peruggia was captured."

"Oh, good. The museum got it back," Beth says.

Ms. Montero's eyes twinkle as if she knows a secret. "Don't be too sure," she says. "At the time, a journalist claimed that Peruggia had been afraid he'd be caught, so he'd destroyed the original, and the *Mona Lisa* that was replaced was another forgery—a very well done forgery, to be sure. The museum denied it, of course."

"Well, was it a forgery?" someone wants to know.

Ms. Montero shrugs. "We may never find out."

"What about the art experts? Can't they tell?"

"Some forgers are so talented that it's very hard for even the experts to tell the copies from the real thing," Ms. Montero explains.

"I have a question," Jonathan says. He asks about security in museums in the United States, but I stop thinking about the *Mona Lisa* theft. That's over and done with. I can't help thinking about what might be another theft. All I can see in my mind is the shining burst of color that hangs in Douglas Merson's entry hall. And Ms. Chase's words, *Douglas has two paintings for the gallery*, echo in my brain. Many trips to Europe . . . paintings brought to an art dealer . . . is Douglas Merson an art thief?

After class I ask Ms. Montero if I can see the slide of Kupka's painting again. I describe the painting, and she knows which one I mean. She reaches into the shelf behind her desk and pulls out a book with photos in it from the Museum of Modern Art in New York. "Here's a photograph of the painting," she says. "It's called *Madame Kupka among Verticals*. Kupka used his wife as his model."

I study the picture carefully. It has to be the very same painting I saw in Douglas Merson's home, but I can't tell Ms. Montero that. I'm not an art expert, so I can't be sure.

"Has this painting ever been . . . well, stolen from the museum?" I ask.

She shakes her head. "Not to my knowledge."

"Is it hanging in the museum now?"

"It should be."

"How do I find out?"

She smiles and says, "You can call the museum and ask."

"Thanks," I tell her. I feel foolish. I should have thought of that myself.

I pick up my books and turn to leave, but she says, "You've made me curious, Kristi. Why do you think the painting might have been stolen?"

She's so nice to me, and she's given me so much encouragement. I have to answer her. "Right now I'm just guessing," I say. "I think I saw that painting in someone's home."

"You probably saw a print."

58

I shake my head. "No. It's oil on canvas. I could see the brush strokes."

"He'd have to be very rich to purchase that painting." She laughs, but I look at her seriously.

"He is."

"Okay," Ms. Montero says. She's not like my parents, who wouldn't give up until they'd learned the whole story, then told me what they thought about it. She smiles at me again and asks, "Do you have the application for the summer art program filled out?"

Slowly I shake my head. I fumble with my books, looking at them as if they're the most interesting things in the world. I can't meet her gaze. "My parents don't want me to go on with art lessons. They think . . . well, that there's not enough money . . . that I'll end up with a degree but no job. I—I tried to talk to them."

"It's all right, Kristi," she says. "If you really want something, you'll work to get it. It might not be in summer school. It might not be in college. But eventually, art can become a very important part of your life."

I raise my head and look into her eyes. "I want to be a professional artist," I say.

Her smile grows even brighter. She answers, "Then I have no doubt that you will be."

As I open the door to leave, Ms. Montero says, "Are you coming to the art club meeting after classes this afternoon? We'll be doing some still-life sketching. I hope you'll join us, Kristi."

"I'll be there," I tell her. Just try to keep me away from what I love to do more than anything else in

59

the whole world. Besides, Jonathan Stockton will probably be there, too.

Jonathan's not only at the meeting, he arrives before I do, so when I walk in, he's already shading in highlights on his sketch of a pear.

"Hi," I say, and I sit at the table next to his as casually as possible.

He looks up briefly. "Hi," he answers, then goes back to his work.

I get my charcoal and art pad ready, then focus on an apple in the arrangement of fruit. The apple's a little misshapen, with only one well-rounded side and a lumpy top that looks like a weird hairstyle. With a few strokes I draw my apple, and it begins to take form as a character. Droopy eyes, a long nose, and a mouth stretched wide, as if he's singing. A few lines here and there, and he has hands and a guitar with one broken string.

I hear a chuckle behind me and look up to see Ms. Montero. "Even without the hat, he's definitely country-western," she says.

Jonathan hesitates, then leans over to look. He doesn't say anything.

"I'm sorry," I tell Ms. Montero as I rip the sheet from my art pad. "I drew what I saw. From now on I'll tend to business."

"I like what you drew," she says. "After all, that's what contemporary art is all about—what the artist sees, how the artist feels. Interpret what you see in your own way, Kristi."

She moves on to see what Beth is doing. I catch Jonathan looking at me. He quickly looks away, then turns back again. "You're good," he says quietly.

Surprised, I say, "I thought you didn't like my drawing."

For the first time Jonathan smiles at me. "I like it. Maybe too much. I guess I'm a little jealous of you, Kristi."

"Jealous?" I realize my mouth is hanging open. With a gulp, I close it.

"It all comes so easy to you," Jonathan says. "I watched you. Just a few quick lines and your apple suddenly was a real character. For a moment I thought I could even tell what he was thinking." He waits a moment, then says, "I can't draw like that. I wish I could."

"Thanks for the compliment," I tell him, "but sometimes I get mad at myself when I get too cartoony. I'd like to sketch like you. Your work is always so well planned. Every line counts."

"I plod at what I do. You don't. You've got a real talent. It must be something you were born with. Heredity. Is either of your parents an artist?"

I shrug. "I didn't get it from my parents. My grandmother says I draw like one of her older brothers, but he was a farmer and didn't have much time to spend on his art. Maybe it just skipped a generation!"

Ms. Montero holds up her left arm and points at her wristwatch. "Watch the time, kids," she says.

The buzz of conversation dies down as we all tend to business. I begin with the best of intentions. But soon a gigantic human hand reaches out over

61

the bowl of fruit, ready to choose something to eat. My apple hunkers down in the bowl, scowling, and my big-bottomed pear winces and grits her teeth. My grapes get into such a pushing-and-shoving match that two of them fall out of the bowl onto the table.

Yeow! Ouch! Look out! I write in balloons coming out of their wide-open mouths. YOU NEED AT LEAST FOUR SERVINGS OF FRUIT A DAY FOR GOOD HEALTH, I print in big letters along the bottom of the page.

Jonathan has inched his stool closer to mine. He looks over my shoulder. "That's very funny. I like it. Could I have it?" he asks.

"Sure," I answer. Then I say, "Let's trade."

He hands me his sketch of a pear. It's beautifully shaded with thin, soft lines. I'd never have that much patience. Every little freckle and bump on the pear has been faithfully sketched in. It's perfect.

And it's dead. I'd like to add closed eyes and a lily in its hand.

But it's Jonathan's. Wonderful, handsome Jonathan. "Thank you," I tell Jonathan, and smile at him, which is very easy to do.

I walk out of class in a happy daze. Jonathan has not only noticed me, he's talked to me. He has even confided in me. But my daydreams about Jonathan disappear with a pop as I reach the bus stop and see a black sedan with someone in it parked halfway down the block.

Same car? No. It couldn't be. There's no license plate in front, and one visor is down. The other car wasn't like that, I'm sure, or I would have noticed. From the long hair and hat it looks as if a woman is

62

sitting in the driver's seat. Just one more black sedan. There must be a million of them.

As I begin to look away the sun glints off whatever the woman is holding, and I quickly glance back. She bends down, as if she's putting something on the seat beside her. What did I see? Why do I have the feeling it was a camera?

The Memorial Drive bus grinds to a stop at the curb, blocking my vision of the car. I climb aboard, and as I settle in a window seat I twist to look back at the car.

It's no longer there. It's nowhere in sight.

Don't start imagining things, I scold myself. *That car and the person inside it had nothing to do with you.*

But I'm really not so sure.

Chapter Seven

//

As I let myself into the house the phone begins to ring. Slamming the kitchen door, I run across the room to answer.

"This is Sergeant Balker, returning your call, Kristi."

"Thanks," I say. "Yesterday I was followed when I was with my friend Lindy. It was a black car—a sedan." I tell him the make and add, "But I got the license plate and—"

"I know. I got the information you left for me, and I followed through. The car belongs to a licensed private investigator. I went to his office this morning and talked with him. He told me he was employed a few months ago by Douglas Merson."

"A few months ago. Then he's the one who took

the recent photographs of me." I think about the glint I saw in the car parked outside school, and the woman in the car. "Does he have a woman working for him too?"

"The guy works alone. He's got a really small operation," Balker answers.

"But I thought the driver today was a woman. Could Mr. Merson have hired more than one person?"

There's a pause, and when Balker speaks I can hear the grin in his voice. "Private eyes on surveillance use all sorts of tricks to disguise their cars and themselves. Sometimes front license plates are snapped off or on. Antennas are put up or down. Both visors down, both up, or one down, one up. The driver changes clothing—hat or sweater, dark glasses on or off, even wigs.

"If you get suspicious about a car that's following close—which it has to in Houston traffic—a few blocks farther on you'll take another look. What do you see? A woman wearing sunglasses has become a man in a baseball cap. No longer both visors up along with an antenna. One visor's down, and the antenna has disappeared. So you decide it's another car, another driver. You stop being suspicious. Just in case you still have that gut feeling that you're being followed, in another mile or so, you'll look for the car, but the identifying marks will have changed again."

I'm glad he's explained. I don't feel quite so stupid now. "Thanks for finding the guy," I say. "Did he tell you why he was hired?"

"No, and I don't think he cared why himself. To

him it's just another job. He doesn't have to keep watch on you or report what you're doing. All he has to do is take pictures."

"Even while Mr. Merson's in the hospital?"

Detective Balker says, "Zigurski claims he didn't know Merson had been shot. All he knows is that he agreed to take a certain number of photos."

"But Mr. Merson can't tell him to stop."

"I told him," Balker says. "I also told him he might not be paid. That seemed to convince him."

"But today . . . this afternoon—he was still doing it, wasn't he?"

"Probably. He's not a very imaginative guy. I'm guessing that all he could think about was the roll of film he wanted to finish, so he could try to get paid in full."

"Are you going to arrest him?"

Balker's voice is quiet and soothing. "Do you really want your parents to press charges, Kristi? Believe me, it will be more trouble than it's worth."

I think about how scared I was, and I wish Sergeant Balker wasn't such a nice guy to everybody.

"Will you give me this private investigator's name? Can I talk to him?" I asked.

"Nope," Balker says. "You don't need to talk to him. And while I'm at it, don't go visiting Merson's neighbors or his hired help anymore."

I gasp with surprise. "Who told you?" I ask, and then I add, "Do you need to mention this to my parents?"

"I'll keep it to myself, but you keep to yourself. Have you got the picture?"

66

"Yes. Completely," I tell him. *Zigurski*. That was the name Balker used a few minutes ago. He doesn't know he had let it slip.

I change the subject. "How is Mr. Merson?"

"Improving," Balker says. "They're going to move him to a private hospital tomorrow."

"Is he still unconscious?"

"What makes you think he was ever unconscious?"

"Um . . ." I try to think of an answer that makes sense, but all I can come up with is, "He was shot."

"He's been doped up and will be for a few more days, but he's conscious. I haven't forgotten what you asked me. When his doctor gives permission, I'll take you to see Merson."

"Thank you," I answer.

"I'll be in touch."

"Wait," I say, remembering the question I haven't found an answer for. "I want to get everything straight. You said Mr. Merson was robbed and shot."

"Right."

"And the thief took his watch."

"Yep. His wallet is missing, too."

"Did the thief go into the house and take anything else?"

"Apparently not. The other occupant of the house reported that he had carefully checked all the rooms. Nothing seemed to be missing."

"Why not? I mean, why wouldn't the thief take the chance to pick up a few more valuable things?"

67

"What are you getting at, Kristi?"

"I don't know."

"Then don't try. It's our job to do the detective work. Okay?"

"Okay," I answer, because right now I really don't know what my question means.

Detective Balker says goodbye in his drawn-out drawl, and I hang up the phone.

I pull a Coke out of the refrigerator and gulp it down while I look under the listing for investigators in the yellow pages. I find R. J. ZIGURSKI, PRIVATE INVESTIGATIONS. Not a big ad. Not even a little ad. Just the last listing in a couple of columns of investigators. I jot down the number and the address, which is almost downtown on San Jacinto Street.

Mom and Dad will be home late, and I'm in charge of dinner. Poking my head into the pantry, I find exactly what I hope is there—a jar of spaghetti sauce and a one-pound package of spaghetti. Nothing in the world is faster to make than spaghetti, when the sauce comes ready-made in a jar. I check my watch. Ten after four. I'm supposed to have dinner ready no later than seven-thirty. If I leave now, I can get to Mr. Zigurski's office before five o'clock. Just to make sure he'll be there, I call his telephone number.

"Zigurski," he says. The phone has an uneven sound, as though he's talking from his car.

"This is Kristi Evans," I tell him. "I can be at your office a little before five o'clock. Will you meet me there?"

He doesn't act surprised to hear from me. His voice is low and flat, with a slight accent that's not

Texan. "No," he answers bluntly. "I'm on assignment."

"But *I'm* your assignment."

"Not anymore, you aren't."

"I was this afternoon. That was you in the car outside my school, wasn't it?"

"Okay, so you made me. That's 'cause you were lookin' to be followed. There were plenty of times when you didn't make me." He sounds defensive, like a kid who goofed on a test.

I get right to the point. "Why did Douglas Merson want you to follow me and take my picture?"

"I dunno. I do what I'm paid to do. I don't ask questions."

"Weren't you curious?"

"I'm not paid to be curious."

"Didn't Mr. Merson say *anything* to you about why he wanted pictures of me?"

For a moment loud static crackles against my ear. Then his voice slides back, flatter than ever. "No, and if he did, do you think I'd tell you?"

"I need to know."

"Tough luck, kid," Mr. Zigurski says, and ends our phone call.

Is Douglas Merson the only one who can tell me the reason for the folder? I can think of one other person who might know about it, since she seems to know Merson well—Ms. Chase.

I turn back to the A–L yellow pages. This time I search through the listing for art galleries, but there's nothing called Chase Galleries. She spoke about *her* gallery. Is she an employee at one of the galleries? Or does she really own an art gallery?

69

From the expensive way she dressed and the car she drove, I'm guessing she's an owner. But what is the gallery's name?

There are more than six columns of listings in the yellow pages. I'll see how many I can eliminate. I take a pencil and go down the columns, crossing out the galleries that don't fit, like the Fine Toon Cartoon Art Gallery. I've been to that gallery, and I love it, but I can't picture Ms. Chase there. There are galleries with small ads that state they specialize in framing prints and photos. I cross them out, along with the galleries with cutesy names. Ms. Chase is definitely elegant, not cutesy. Last, I cross out the galleries that carry the names of the owners. I'm betting on Ms. Chase being the owner.

I'm still left with a long list to call, so I sit down with the telephone and get to work. I don't want to talk to Ms. Chase on the phone. She could put me off as easily as Mr. Zigurski did. So when someone answers my first call, I don't ask to speak to Ms. Chase. I just say, "Could you please tell me if Ms. Chase works at this gallery?"

"No, she doesn't. Sorry," the voice says, and the person hangs up.

"Ms. Who?" the second voice asks.

But the woman on the phone at the third gallery says, "Are you looking for Alanna Chase?"

"I think so. Tall, dark-haired, very attractive—" I begin.

The woman makes some kind of noise I can't quite figure out—sort of a snort or grunt. "Alanna's an owner of the Royal Heritage Gallery of Art," she tells me.

Royal Heritage. If Alanna named the gallery herself, I should have figured that one out. "Thank you," I answer. "I appreciate your help." Excitement swells like a bubble in my chest.

The Royal Heritage Gallery of Art is listed in the phone book. I circle the name and copy down its phone number and address. It's on Westheimer, close to the Galleria. It won't take me long to get there.

I check the garage, and Mom's car is parked inside, just as I'd hoped. She and Dad have been keeping the same long hours, working hard to finish their clients' income taxes on time, so they've been driving to their office together. I don't bother to leave a note telling them where I'm going. I'll get home long before they do. I take a small notebook and pen with me, just in case I need them.

When I arrive at the address I miss the drive and have to circle the block. I look for a gallery sign, and there isn't one. Instead, there's a tall office building. I manage to find a parking slot in the covered parking area behind the building and enter the lobby.

I find myself swimming in a vast pool of reflected light that shimmers over sea-green marble flooring and walls. A receptionist with long hair sits behind a low mahogany desk at a far end of the room. She's the only human being in sight. With soft, piped-in music surrounding me, I walk to her desk and ask, "Where will I find the Royal Heritage Gallery of Art?"

"Seventeenth floor, suite seventeen hundred," she tells me in a clipped Eastern accent.

"Thank you," I say. At the elevator bank I punch a button to summon an elevator and am soon whisked to the seventeenth floor so fast that my ears pop.

I've gone from the sea to a sand dune. As I cross the lobby I sink to my ankles—well, maybe my toes—in a pale cream-colored carpet. It's the thickest I've ever seen. Across from me three large white canvases, each surrounded with a thin line of color—one red, one green, and one blue—hang on the wall. The frames are expensive, but the art does nothing for me.

Only one door leads into this lobby. It's a beautifully carved double door to my left. Fastened to it is a brass plate with the name of Ms. Chase's gallery.

The door is closed. I try the handle, but it's locked, so I knock.

A buzzer blasts over my head. It startles me so much that I jump. It sounds again. It must mean I can open the door, so once more I try the handle. This time it turns easily.

As I enter the room I gasp with surprise. The gallery consists of a series of rooms with stark white walls and dividers. The lighting is clear and bright, highlighting rows and rows of paintings. I'm surrounded by contemporary art, and in the room beyond I see soft landscapes that remind me of John Constable's.

"Do you have an appointment?" a voice asks.

I quickly turn to see a thin, long-faced man standing next to me. Everything about him is thin,

72

from his nose to his hair. He's escaped from an El Greco painting.

"I don't have an appointment," I answer, "but I'd like to see Ms. Chase, if I may. Just for a few minutes, please."

"May I ask the nature of your business?" He's very solemn and businesslike. He glances pointedly at my notebook.

I go along with the game and try to act every bit as dignified as he. There's no point in making up an excuse, but I'm not sure how much of my story to tell him. I keep it brief. "My name is Kristin Evans. I would like to talk to Ms. Chase, please."

"Ms. Chase is extremely busy. Suppose you talk to me."

"No, really, I need to talk to Ms. Chase. It's important."

His mouth twists in a dry smile. "Let me guess. You wish Ms. Chase to speak to your art class. Or donate a small print to your school library's silent auction." He claps one hand to his face. "Oh, now I know. You wish to purchase a painting."

I don't like his sarcasm. I don't like him. But I stay calm.

"I wish to speak to her about Mr. Douglas Merson."

Both of his eyebrows rise slightly. Merson's name certainly got his attention. "What about Douglas Merson?" he asks.

How do I get past this man? All I can do is tell the truth and hope he gives in. "Mr. Merson was shot Saturday night. Ms. Chase is a friend of his. I

73

just need to know something about Mr. Merson, and I hope she can tell me."

He studies me for a moment. Then he relaxes, and I catch a look of mischievous humor in his eyes. "As if the media itself isn't a problem, now they're sending in the junior media," he says. "Please wait here. I'll convey your message to Ms. Chase."

What's so funny? I wish I could ask him, but I don't.

He walks toward the back of the gallery. I should have asked him if I could look around while I'm waiting, but I forgot. I try to catch up with him, but he doesn't notice, and the soft carpet muffles my footsteps. I'm too late. He opens a door and walks through. It doesn't completely close behind him.

A woman's voice rises shrilly. "I just got off the phone. I was right, Landreth. They're getting close, and he's ready to cooperate, just as he threatened. Do you know what this will mean? He must be out of his mind."

"We have a visitor," I hear Landreth caution. In a low voice he says, "I told you, there's no need to worry."

Her voice drops and she answers, "He'll plea-bargain. He'll blame—" But I've already walked away. I hope she'll talk to me.

I hurry to the main room, to see the paintings. The first is a mixture of swirls and bursts with a touch of cubism. *The Party*, it's titled. It's an interesting painting, and the artist must have had a great time at the party, but he doesn't breathe the fire of Frank Kupka.

74

The next painting is an explosion of color radiating from the center. It reminds me of Boccioni's *Dynamism of a Soccer Player*, but without the intensity and tremendous energy. *Lydia*, the painting is called. *Wow, Lydia! Did you ever make a great impression!* I think. I bend to read the artist's name. Same artist. I haven't heard of him, but that doesn't mean anything. *You're pretty good*, I tell him. *You're on your way, but you need practice. Or maybe a soul. Lydia should have a soul. Did you look for it? You've left her soul out of this piece.*

This is great fun. I'm not only a world-renowned art critic, I'm a gallery owner too. This is my very own gallery—The Heavens by Evans. *Yes, ladies and gentlemen, I live to encourage young artists. At my own great expense I send them to art school when their parents won't. And I—*

"Yes? You asked to see me?"

I turn and look into the carefully designed face of Alanna Chase. This time she's actually seeing me. Her eyes are slightly narrowed as if she's a little suspicious. Maybe I'm the first teenager to set foot in her gallery. I can see that she doesn't remember me from yesterday. Lindy and I were totally unimportant to her so she mentally wiped us out.

"*You're* Ms. Evans? You're only a child," she says. She doesn't try to hide her irritation. She glances around, but the man who took my message to her is nowhere in sight. Now I know why he was smiling, but I don't care. I've gotten my meeting.

"My name is Kristin Evans," I say.

"So you told Landreth," she snaps. My name hasn't registered with her.

"I'm hoping that Mr. Merson told you about me."

"Well, he didn't," she says. Then she cocks her head like a grackle studying a worm. "Why should he?"

"That's what I was hoping you'd tell me," I answer.

Ms. Chase's lips tighten, and she looks at the gold and diamond watch on her left wrist. "I don't have time to play silly guessing games. You have two minutes in which to tell me the purpose of your visit."

I'd love to ask her about some of the paintings. I'd love to be able to walk through the gallery rooms and explore the art. Right now, I take a deep breath and say, "Please tell me what you know about Mr. Merson. What is he like? What does he do for a living? Why does he travel so often to Europe? Does he import art for your gallery?"

Ms. Chase holds up a hand—her rings glittering—and momentarily closes her eyes. "Stop!" she demands. "Who do you think you are, prying into someone's life? Do you honestly expect me to confide details of Douglas's life to you—not only a child, but a total stranger?"

There's no use trying to explain, so I simply say, "He's kept a folder of clippings and photos of me for sixteen years. I have to know why. Maybe I can find out by learning who Douglas Merson really is."

Ms. Chase's look becomes even more wary. She says, "Because of the contents of that alleged folder, I suppose you feel you have some sort of claim on Douglas."

"A claim?" That's a strange thing to say. "Oh, no," I tell her. "I don't even know Mr. Merson."

"You and your parents have no idea why he kept this file on you—assuming you're telling the truth and he did?"

"No. I'd hoped he could tell me." I can't help sighing. "His face was bandaged. I couldn't even tell what he looked like."

She steps toward me with such fierceness that I stumble backward. Thrusting her face into mine, she growls, "*You* saw Douglas? They let *you* in to see him?"

"No!" I tell her. "I tried. I mean I got in, but a nurse asked me to leave."

It was a big mistake to mention going to the hospital. Ms. Chase is shaking, and the darkness behind her eyes frightens me. "What did Douglas say to you?" she demands.

I shake my head. "Nothing. He couldn't talk. He was totally out of it."

Ms. Chase steps back, breathing heavily. I can see her trying to gain control of herself, picking up all the little pieces that exploded in anger and fitting them back where they belong.

Finally she says, "You're a very foolish girl. Someone tried to kill Douglas. Don't you realize that the person may try again? Douglas is still in great danger. You should keep away for your sake as well."

Her eyes drill into mine as she adds, "For your own safety, Ms. Evans, stay away from him, and stop asking so many nosy questions or you could find yourself in danger too."

77

CHAPTER EIGHT

//

The minute I walk into the safety of my own kitchen, I dump my books on the table. I go to the telephone and get the number for the Museum of Modern Art in New York City. I'm finally connected to someone who, I hope, can answer my question. "Is the painting *Madame Kupka among Verticals* by Frank Kupka on display?"

"Not at the present time," she says.

I know that sometimes museums lend their paintings to special exhibitions at other museums. Maybe that's where the Kupka work is. But in my mind I see those glorious strips of color hanging in Douglas Merson's entry hall. I have to ask. "Where is the painting? Is it on loan? Can you tell me?"

The line is silent for a moment. Then she says, "Who is this?"

"I just need to know if the painting has been stolen," I tell her. I realize I must sound like a nut.

Her voice takes on a strange tone. "Stay on the line. I'm going to transfer your call to our security department," she says.

Maybe she does. I don't know. I hang up, nearly dropping the phone because my fingers are trembling.

I have to admit that I'm a little scared. I wish I could talk to Mom and Dad about what's going on, but at this time of year they come home from the office exhausted, gulp down their dinner, and go back to work until very late at night. I know from experience that after April 15, when even the last-minute clients have their income tax returns in the mail, Mom and Dad will turn into real people again, but by then it may be too late.

When Ms. Chase told me Mr. Merson was in danger, I realized she was right. There must have been something about the robbery that frightened the thief. Did he think Mr. Merson could identify him? Is that why he shot him? If that's the reason, whoever tried to kill Mr. Merson might keep trying. Does my folder fit in, or is that just coincidence?

I take Sergeant Balker's card from my wallet and phone him. This time he answers the call himself. I can hear a voice on an intercom in the background: "Will Dr. Harvey Walters please report to pediatrics?"

"Are you in a hospital?" I ask Balker.

"That's right," he answers.

"With Mr. Merson? Or somebody else?"

"Hey, Kristi, does it matter?"

"I think it does," I say, "because somebody tried to kill Mr. Merson and may have tried to make it look like a robbery. Maybe Mr. Merson knows who it was and can tell you as soon as he can talk. Okay? So the person may try again to kill him before he gets the chance." I run out of breath, so I gulp in a lungful of air. "I thought you ought to know."

"It occurred to us," Balker drawls. "We're on top of the situation."

"Are you with Mr. Merson now?"

The call goes out on the intercom again: "Will Dr. Harvey Walters please report to pediatrics?"

Balker raises his voice, speaking over it. "As a matter of fact, I just talked to Merson. Are you satisfied?"

"Did he tell you who shot him?" I ask.

"He can't speak. Remember?"

"Can he write? Can he draw a picture of the killer?"

Balker chuckles. "Want to be a detective when you grow up, Kristi? You're on the right track."

I gasp. "Who did he say shot him?"

There's just a slight pause before Balker says, "You'll hear it from the media anyway, so I can tell you this much. Merson opened the door to someone in a ski mask. The porch light had been shattered, and the house is set back from the street, so there wasn't enough light for him to make out any distinguishing details. Then everything happened fast."

80

"But was the person in the mask tall or short? Was it a man or a woman?"

"He doesn't know. He couldn't tell. As I said, it was dark and everything came down in a hurry."

"Do you have a policeman stationed there to protect him in case the robber comes back to keep Mr. Merson from identifying him?"

"All Merson saw was the ski mask. Kristi, you watch too many cop shows on TV."

"Someone has to be with Mr. Merson."

"If Merson is concerned he can get the guy who works for him to hire a bodyguard. That's up to him."

I visualize Merson as I saw him, wrapped in bandages, attached to tubes, and lying helpless in bed. I'm swept with a new surge of pity for him, even though I don't really know who he is. "May I please come and visit Mr. Merson now?" I ask.

"Not just yet. Give it a few days."

I feel strange about asking. My face grows hot as I mumble, "Did he . . . well, did he say anything about me?"

"No, and I didn't ask him. The doctor limited my time to ask questions."

"What hospital is Mr. Merson in?"

Balker laughs again. "Nice try, Kristi, but it won't work. As I promised, I'll be in touch with you. I'll take you and your parents to see Merson when the time is right. You'll have to be satisfied with that."

"Okay," I answer. There's no point in arguing— especially not when I know how to find out the name of the hospital.

I pick up the yellow pages again and turn to the hospitals section. I can't believe there are so many hospitals in Houston.

For a moment I'm angry with Detective Balker for not just telling me where Mr. Merson is. It would save me a lot of work.

I take Jonathan's drawing of a pear from my notebook and place it on the kitchen counter, near the phone, where it will be safe from splatters. Jonathan drew it. Jonathan gave it to me, so it doesn't matter that the pear never had a chance to live. I'll never bury it. Instead, I'll tape it on the mirror in my bedroom.

Mom and Dad arrive home. As I begin to dish up the spaghetti and the salad of mixed field greens that I've tossed together, Dad stops at the counter and picks up the drawing. "Callie! Look at this pear!" he exclaims, excitement in his voice. "This is great. This looks just like a real pear." He beams at me. "Kristi, you don't need art lessons. You've got a natural talent."

I ache inside. "It's not my drawing, Dad," I say quietly. "A friend of mine gave it to me."

"Oh," Dad says. As he puts down the drawing, he looks embarrassed. "Well, your friend has real talent . . . too," he adds.

During dinner Mom and Dad try to talk to me about school and stuff that I'm doing, but I don't feel like talking. There's too much to think about. They've always made it easy for me to talk about anything with them, so I feel a little guilty that now I can't. Finally they give up trying to reach me and discuss their clients' tax problems. As soon as they've finished eating and head for their home office and their computers, I sit down with the telephone and the yellow pages.

I choose the biggest hospitals first, then move to some of the smaller private ones between River Oaks and the Medical Center. In each case I ask for the pediatrics department. When someone answers, I ask for Dr. Harvey Walters.

It's not until late the next afternoon, on my second try, that I get what I want. The receptionist answers me by saying, "Dr. Walters has left Riverview for the day. Please call his office. Do you have that number?"

"Yes, thank you," I say quickly, and hang up.

Riverview Hospital. It's on Woodway. I write down the address and tuck the slip of paper into my bag. As soon as I can I'm going to pay another visit to Douglas Merson.

———— // ————

On Wednesday I get up a half hour early and have breakfast on the table when Mom and Dad come into the kitchen. They look at the platters of scrambled eggs, sliced melon, and buttered toast and smile with delight.

Mom hugs me, and I ache when I see the dark circles under her eyes. "You and Dad need to eat a good breakfast," I tell her. "Coffee and toast doesn't cut it."

"Who's the mother?" she teases me.

"Whoever makes breakfast." I grin.

It's pretty quiet as they begin to eat, but I break

the silence. "I talked to Sergeant Balker yesterday. He said Mr. Merson has been moved to a private hospital."

Dad and Mom both look up quickly.

"Did he say which one?" Dad asks.

"Sergeant Balker didn't tell me anything," I say, "except that Mr. Merson didn't see the person who shot him. There's no way he can identify him."

"Mr. Merson can talk?" Mom asks.

"No, but I guess he can write."

"Good," she says firmly. She bites down hard on her toast and chews it as though she's crushing it to death. "He has some explaining to do to us. At this time of the year we need all the sleep we can get. I don't appreciate having to lie awake nights worrying about what peculiar interest some strange man has in our daughter!"

I reach across the table and pat her hand. "Mom, Sergeant Balker said he'd take us to see Mr. Merson in just a few days."

"Did he say what day?" Dad asks.

"No. I don't think he knows yet."

Mom peers at the tiny calendar fastened to the band on her wristwatch. "It's going to have to be on a Sunday. There's no way your father and I can take off during the week." She gives a little moan. "But I do need to know what this is all about."

"Don't worry, Mom. You will. The police are right on top of it."

And so am I. But I don't need to tell them that.

———— // ————

84

Art appreciation class is great, as usual. Ms. Montero is taking us through some really fascinating art history. As I study the slides on the screen I itch to visit the museums in person. Oh, if only I were an art historian myself, I'd get lost in the galleries and churches of Rome!

Ms. Montero turns off the projector and flips on the lights. "On Friday evening at seven-thirty there's a preview showing of an exhibition of eighteenth-century French paintings at the Museum of Fine Arts. Two of the paintings you just saw will be in the exhibit. I've arranged to get tickets for those of you who'd like to attend for extra credit."

I wave my hand wildly as she writes down names. I can't wait to go.

Jonathan stops by my desk as the class ends. His voice is softer than usual, and he stares at the floor. "We could go to the exhibition together," he says.

My heart gives a jump. All along I've thought Jonathan wasn't interested in me, but that wasn't it. Jonathan's shy.

His shyness is contagious. I find myself stammering, groping for words. I can feel my face turn red. "Uh—sure. I would. I mean, I'd like that. Going together, that is."

"Okay," Jonathan says. He stops looking at my shoes. He raises his gaze until he's looking right into my eyes, and he smiles at me. "I'll pick you up at seven."

I smile back. I don't try to talk because my insides have turned squishy. Jonathan Stockton is the best-looking guy I've ever seen. And he's asked me for a date. Well, sort of a date. Through the rest of the day I float on invisible wings and sketch little Jonathans along the margins in my notebook. I can't wait to tell Lindy. She doesn't care about art, but she'll care about my date.

———————//———————

When I reach home after school, the wings fall off and I land with a thud. There's a message from Mom on the answering machine.

"Detective Balker called. He's arranging for you, Dad, and me to visit Douglas Merson on Sunday afternoon." There's a pause, and Mom's voice drops, as if she's talking to herself. "He didn't say what hospital, and I didn't think to ask him. Oh, well, it's only Wednesday. He'll be in touch with us before Sunday." She picks up speed again and adds, "I took a package of ground beef out of the freezer and put it into the refrigerator. Be sure you defrost it completely in the microwave. You'll find a package of mushrooms in the refrigerator. They're getting a little too soft to be used in salad, so make a meat loaf for dinner, along with sautéed mushrooms and whatever else you want. Thanks, honey, for being such a big help. We'll be home between seven-thirty and eight."

The recording clicks off, and I lean against the counter with a sigh. Sunday? We can't see Douglas Merson until Sunday?

Maybe Mom and Dad can wait that long, but I can't. I'm going to visit Mr. Merson right now.

It takes only a little over fifteen minutes to drive

to Riverview Hospital, find a parking place shaded by tall pine trees, and ask at the reception desk the number of Mr. Merson's room. The white-haired volunteer in the pink hospital uniform has such a friendly smile, she reminds me of Grandma, and I feel a sudden pang of longing for my grandmother. I wish she lived nearby and I could see her more than two or three times a year. Grandma would agree that I should study to become an artist. If there are sides to be taken, Grandma's always on mine.

"Sixth floor," the volunteer says. "Room six fifty-five. You can get further directions from a floor nurse at the central desk on the sixth floor. The elevators are to your right."

"Thank you," I say, and take the nearest elevator, which dings and slides its doors open as I approach.

On the sixth floor there's a sign with room numbers and arrows on it, so I don't have any trouble finding Mr. Merson's room. Six fifty-five is at the end of the hallway to my right, next to the last door, which is labeled EXIT—STAIRS.

Mr. Merson's door stands ajar, so I peek inside. The room is flooded with late afternoon's intense light, which pours through the open venetian blinds. This is a large room, with plenty of space for the two upholstered armchairs, the usual hospital bed, and bedside tables.

Mr. Merson, still bandaged and connected to tubes and machines, is lying there quietly, his eyes closed. He seems to be peacefully asleep.

I back away from the door and walk past the exit to a small alcove at the end of the hallway, where I lean against the wall and think about what to do next. Mr. Merson has been badly hurt. He's in pain. He needs to sleep . . . to heal. How could I possibly wake him? The detectives will be mad. My parents will be shocked that I came here—but I realize I've been doing lots of things my parents would find shocking. I haven't felt ashamed, though.

My need to know who he is and why he's had this sixteen-year interest in me is not selfish. I could leave him undisturbed. I could come back Sunday, when I'm with Mom and Dad and Detective Balker. But what really is fair?

I straighten just as the door to the stairs begins to open. It moves only a few inches, then stops. I don't hear a sound from the other side of the door, so I realize that it's not someone struggling to carry something through the door. It's someone who seems to be waiting quietly, holding the door open just wide enough to look through. Since I'm standing on the hinged side of the door, I can't see who's there.

I hear two women's voices as they come down the hall toward us. Their chatter rises to a squeal. "Annabelle! You're looking wonderful!" A door closes behind them as they enter Annabelle's room, and the hall is empty again.

Now the stair door opens wide, and someone comes through. As it closes, I get a quick glimpse of a doctor in a loose green cotton top and pants, cotton cap completely covering his hair, and even a surgical mask tied across his face. He looks as if he just walked out of an operating room on a TV show. In a few steps he reaches the door of Mr. Merson's room and enters.

Weird, I think. *Something about all this isn't right.* I'm pretty sure that doctors don't leave surgery when dressed like that and then go visiting patients in their rooms.

I walk to Mr. Merson's door, which is shut now. I grip the handle and slowly open the door.

Blinking, I can barely make out shapes in the room. The blinds and drapes have been closed, turning the once-bright room into a dark cavern. The doctor is bending over Mr. Merson's bed, a large pillow in his hands.

In bed Mr. Merson twists and struggles. His muffled moan terrifies me, but I yell at the doctor. "What are you doing?" I run toward him, shouting, "Put down that pillow! Take that off his face!"

The figure whirls and swings the pillow at my head. He shoves me in the chest so that I stagger backward, hit the wall, and fall to the floor.

As he dashes out the door I manage to get to my feet then into the hall, but he's disappeared.

"Help!" I yell, and nurses pop out from their center station. "Help! Someone tried to kill Mr. Merson!"

CHAPTER NINE

//

People appear from everywhere. I explain to a uniformed security guard about the doctor who tried to smother Mr. Merson, and he heads for the stairs. I tell the story over and over to nurses and doctors and people in business suits.

"No, I didn't get a close look at the doctor," I say. "The room was dark. The doctor shoved me against the wall."

"You didn't get a good look at his eyes?"

"No."

"Did you notice any unusual identifying marks?"

"I told you, the room was too dark."

"How tall was he?"

"I'm not sure. Average height, I guess . . . No.

Maybe taller. I think he was a little bit taller than I am."

"Color of hair?"

"I don't know. The hospital cap covered all of it."

"Male or female?"

"I don't know!"

Finally the questions stop. I realize that most of the people have left, and those going in and around Mr. Merson's room are now moving normally and quietly. The security guard informs me that a hospital scrub suit like the one I described was found on the second-floor landing. He holds it up, and I identify it as like the one the attacker was wearing.

The security guard takes my name. Then a nurse asks if I'm hurt. She tells me Mr. Merson wants to see me.

"How is he?" I ask.

"He's fine," she says.

I can't believe her matter-of-fact attitude at a time like this. "He's fine? After almost being murdered?"

"He was upset, but his blood pressure has returned to normal and his vital signs are good."

She leads me into his room, cheerfully chirping, "Here she is, Mr. Merson. Here's the young lady who chased away your attacker."

"Hello," I say to this stranger I have been waiting eagerly to meet, "I'm Kristi Evans."

He raises his left hand and points toward one of the armchairs. Then he motions as though he wants it moved closer.

I push the armchair close to the side of his bed and sit in it. Again he reaches out with his hand, and I think I know what he means. I hold out my left hand and clasp his in a backward handshake.

I'm wrong. That's not what he wants. He turns my hand so that it's resting on the blanket cover, palm up. Then, with his index finger, he draws the shape of letters in my palm, T-H-A-N-K Y-O-U.

I tell him, "A person you know, Ms. Chase, said that whoever tried to kill you might come back and try again."

His eyebrows rise, and I answer the questions in his eyes. "I went to your house. She came while I was there. She told Frederick she wanted to pick up some paintings you had promised her."

Once again his eyebrows rise and fall. I say, "Detectives came to our house Sunday because they'd found the folder you've been keeping about me."

I pause, waiting for him to respond, but he lies there quietly looking at me. Finally he prints in my palm, G-O O-N.

"Okay," I say, giving in for the moment. "I'll go first, but I need questions answered, and I'm getting tired of waiting."

So I tell Mr. Merson about visiting the intensive care unit soon after he was taken to Ben Taub. "You didn't know it, but I was there."

He shakes his head, then nods.

"What? You did know?"

He nods again.

"I thought you were sedated."

Once more he nods.

92

"You mean you could hear what I said, even though you were out of it?"

He traces the letters in my hand. I H-E-A-R-D Y-O-U.

I look him straight in the eyes. "Then you know why I came. I have to know who you are. I have to know why you kept a folder of clippings and photographs about me."

He writes in my palm again, and I hold my breath, concentrating intently. All he writes is G-O O-N.

Reluctantly I answer, "I said I'd talk first, so I will, in order of how it happened."

I describe going to his house and talking to Frederick and seeing Ms. Chase for the first time.

"I saw Frank Kupka's painting of his wife 'among verticals' hanging in your entry hall," I tell him.

I wait for the look of alarm when he realizes that the painting has been recognized, but instead his eyes glow with pleasure. What do I say next? I can't tell him I know where the painting rightfully belongs.

I interrupt the logical flow and ask, "Do you own other artists' paintings?"

He nods.

"I'd love to see them."

He writes in my hand, C-O-M-E.

"I will," I tell him. But I take a quick breath as a sudden thought disturbs me. Will the paintings be his own property? Or will they belong to someone else?

Mr. Merson is waiting, so I get back to my story. I tell him about being followed and what Sergeant

Balker found out about the private investigator. Last, I tell him about tracking down Ms. Chase and visiting her art gallery.

His eyes crinkle, and I hear a low chuckle in the back of his throat.

"I'm going to call Detective Balker when I get home," I promise. "I'm going to try to get him to assign someone to protect you."

A voice speaks from the doorway. I look up to see Detective Nims. "You don't have to call Detective Balker," she says. "The hospital informed us of what happened here."

"Are you going to put a policeman on guard?" I ask.

"Temporarily," she says. "While we're doing our investigation. You don't need to help us, Kristi."

"Do you mean until you find and arrest the person who tried to murder Mr. Merson?"

"We can't make a promise for a scope as wide as that," she says. "You can leave now, Kristi. I have some questions to ask Mr. Merson." She pulls a pad and pencil from her bag. "You can write the answers on this," she tells him.

Mr. Merson clasps my hand tightly. Then his finger traces two letters in my palm.

"He wrote 'N-O' in my hand," I tell her. "He doesn't want me to leave, and he doesn't want to answer questions."

Detective Nims frowns and moves to my chair. She hovers over me and makes it clear that I have no choice about staying or going. "Mr. Merson," she says, "Kristi is scheduled to visit you here at the hospital with her parents and Sergeant Balker on Sunday afternoon. You'll see her then."

"But there's something he was going to tell me," I complain.

"He'll have to do it next time," she says firmly.

I stand up to leave, sliding my hand away from Mr. Merson's. He sends me a pleading look. "I'll be back," I promise. "I really will."

The door opens and Ms. Chase sails into the room. Ms. Chase holds a bowl that contains a huge arrangement of yellow tulips mixed with sprays of white dogwood. Ignoring Detective Nims and me, she plops the arrangement down on the wide windowsill, then rushes to Mr. Merson's bedside.

"Douglas, it's me, Alanna," she says loudly, as though Mr. Merson has gone deaf. "Do you recognize me? Can you see who I am?"

Mr. Merson nods, and Sergeant Nims says, "According to the doctors, his mind is clear, and he hasn't experienced any damage to his eyesight . . . or any loss of hearing."

Ms. Chase turns to look at Sergeant Nims with irritation. Nims introduces herself and adds, "I was about to question Mr. Merson. You may return to his room when I've finished. There's a waiting room near the elevators."

"Haven't you already questioned him?" Ms. Chase snaps. "Why are you pestering the poor darling?"

Nims says, "A short time ago another attempt was made on Mr. Merson's life."

"Here in the hospital?"

95

"Exactly."

Ms. Chase gasps, slaps a hand over her heart, and staggers into the armchair. "Another attempt? Here? But it can't be! Oh, Douglas!"

"You said someone probably would try again to kill him," I tell her. "You were right."

Nims gives me a sharp look, then quickly turns it on Ms. Chase. "What do you know about this attack?"

Ms. Chase glares at me. "I simply told this young lady that whoever tried to kill Douglas during the robbery at his home might try again, if he thought Douglas had recognized him."

"Yes. That's what she said," I tell Nims.

Ms. Chase sits upright and looks at Mr. Merson with concern. "*Did* you recognize him, Douglas?" she asks. "Could you identify him?"

We all stare at Mr. Merson, waiting for his answer. He sighs, closes his eyes, then shakes his head.

His eyes slowly open. He motions to me to come near.

When I do he takes one of my hands and writes, T-I-R-E-D. G-O.

"He's tired," I say. "He wants us all to go away and let him rest."

"A wise idea," the nurse who is now in the room says. "I was about to inform you myself that visiting time is over."

Ms. Chase jumps up, trots to the foot of the bed, and begins to question Sergeant Nims about police protection.

I'm puzzled by my strange feelings as I look down at this man, whose face I still haven't seen. Although he seems to know all about me, I don't know anything about him. No one seems to know anything. From what I've guessed, he might be an art thief. I've even been told that he's suspected of being a drug dealer. And yet I want to like him.

"Goodbye, Mr. Merson," I say quietly, and try to slip my hand from his, but he holds it tightly. His gaze is compelling as he prints in my hand, C-O-M-E S-O-O-N.

"Yes," I murmur. "I'll see you soon."

As I walk to the door Ms. Chase says loudly, "Douglas, dear, we're going to get you a bodyguard. I'll speak to Frederick. I'll hire one myself."

I'm glad she offered. She may be flaky, but she's still a good friend to hire protection for him. And isn't that what friends are all about—coming through for you when you need them the most? I look at my watch. Thinking about good friends makes me think of Lindy. As soon as I get home and start dinner, I'll call her and tell her the latest.

A young doctor, dressed in a white coat, with a stethoscope draped around his neck, walks up to me as I wait for an elevator. "Kristin Evans?" he asks me.

"Yes," I tell him.

"I'm Dr. Lynd, on the hospital staff, now Mr. Merson's primary physician. I asked one of the nurses to point you out. Mr. Merson has been writing notes, asking for you."

That surprises me because no one has told me, but I say, "I'm supposed to come on Sunday

97

with my parents, but I didn't want to wait that long."

He grins. "Your timing was great. It looks like you arrived at just the right time. Are you his granddaughter?"

"Mr. Merson's not my grandfather," I tell him.

"I guess I just took it for granted . . . his age . . . yours . . ."

"He's . . . well, he's . . . a friend," I say.

"Fine. That's exactly what Mr. Merson needs right now," the doctor says. "When a patient feels well in mind and spirit, it helps him recover faster. I hope you'll come back."

"I'll come back soon," I answer.

"Good. I like my patients to get well." Dr. Lynd smiles.

The elevator comes, and I step into it. As the doors close, I think about my mother's father, Grandpa Bill, who died when I was twelve. I still miss him. And I think about Dad's father. I never got to meet him. Dad's parents died in a car accident when Dad was in his teens.

For an instant I wish Mr. Merson *were* my grandfather.

On the way home I turn on my favorite radio station and try to blast away my anxiety. I can't help wondering why the killer came back.

Did he think Mr. Merson could identify him?

Or was there another reason?

Mentally I go over stories about murders that have been in the news. I remember someone killing a witness because he was afraid the man would testify against him. In some murders, people gave in to a terrible anger. One case, I remember, had to do with greed. Some of the worst murders took place because of revenge.

Someone out there is trying to kill Mr. Merson, and no one but the would-be killer himself knows who he is or why he wants to commit murder.

Shuddering, I turn the radio up.

CHAPTER TEN

———— // ————

While the meat loaf is in the oven I call Lindy. I have so much to tell her.

"Mr. Merson actually heard you talking to him while he was in intensive care?" she exclaims. "What did you say? Do you remember?"

"I only had a short time before the nurse told me to leave. I remember that I explained who I was and said I knew about the folder. I asked Mr. Merson who *he* was."

Lindy's voice rises in excitement. "Did he tell you? I mean, not then, but now . . . today . . . when you visited him?"

I sigh with frustration. "I think he was going to. He wanted to know about me first, so I told him. But then Detective Nims came into the room and

106

ordered me to leave. She wanted to ask Mr. Merson some questions."

Lindy gives a sympathetic groan. "No fair. She could have waited."

"I guess I'm the one who'll have to wait. Maybe he'll tell us on Sunday when Mom and Dad come to see him too."

"You'll call me right away, won't you? I mean, the very minute you get back home? I'm dying of curiosity."

"You know I will," I promise. I find myself saying, "I spoke with this one doctor who told me that Mr. Merson had asked about me. He took it for granted that Mr. Merson was my grandfather."

"Probably because Mr. Merson's so old," Lindy answers. "Speaking about grandparents reminds me . . ." She begins to complain about the report she has to write for her community issues and ethics class. "I was going to write about grandparents as parents. Lots of kids are being raised by grandparents because of single-parent families and families where both parents work, but Angie Stone already picked that topic. Julie chose teen moms, Andy's got something about affirmative action, and Jonathan has test-tube babies. There isn't anything really good left! Any ideas?"

I search for an answer and, thankfully, an idea pops into my mind. "Why don't you write about child advocates? You know, the people who volunteer to stand up for kids and their rights when the kids or their parents are in court?"

"Hey, that's good!" Lindy says. "There's even a big group called Child Advocates in Houston. I know because their ads are in the *Chronicle*. I'll bet they'll give me tons of information."

Lindy rattles on, but my mind goes in another direction. "Did you say Jonathan is in your class?" I interrupt.

"Yes, your boyfriend is in the class too," she teases.

"He's not my boyfriend," I reply, but I have to admit I do like the way it sounds.

"Not yet," says Lindy, "but after your big date this weekend he may be. So have you thought about what you're going to wear?"

We quickly go over a few outfits, but before we can decide on anything, I hear Dad's car drive up and the garage door crank open. "I've got to go," I tell Lindy. "Mom and Dad are home. I'll see you tomorrow."

Mom kicks off her shoes, washes her hands, and works beside me as I finish making dinner. Dad changes and comes back into the kitchen in comfortable clothes. "What can I do?" he asks.

"You can pour the water," Mom says. At the same time, she and I both reach for the buttered, seasoned bread crumbs to put on the tomatoes we're going to broil. We collide. Laughing, we make a second try, and Dad says, "That reminds me of a joke I heard about two mountain climbers."

We listen and groan. I don't know where Dad finds these corny jokes.

I wait to tell Mom and Dad what happened at the hospital.

Dad settles back in his chair and smiles. "You're a good cook, Kristi," he says.

102

"It's just plain old meat loaf," I answer. "Nothing special."

"Maybe it's what you put with it. The broiled tomatoes were good, and I like the salad with pecans in it."

"Mom made the tomatoes."

Mom pats my hand and smiles too. Food energy is kicking in. They're perking up. Now's the time, I decide, to tell them.

"Did you have a good day, honey?" Mom asks me.

"It was an unusual day," I say. I take a deep breath and go through the story of what happened at the hospital with Mr. Merson.

Neither Mom nor Dad interrupts. They listen with wide eyes until I reach the end. Then the questions start.

"Why couldn't you wait until Sunday, when we'll be with you?" Mom asks. "That maniac could have killed you, too!"

"I didn't know what was going to happen. Anyhow, he didn't kill me. And because I was there he didn't kill Mr. Merson, either."

"That's beside the point. We don't know Mr. Merson. We don't know what kind of a person he is. It was a brave thing for you to do, but you shouldn't have been there without us."

"What had you hoped to accomplish by visiting him, Kristi?" Dad asks.

I sigh. "I hoped to find out who Mr. Merson is," I answer. "I didn't. But I *did* accomplish something. I saved his life."

"Granted," he says. "And we're proud of you for

103

that, but we worry that you're taking dangerous options."

I lean toward them, looking from one to the other. "Let me ask a question now. It's about my birth."

I can see Mom's shoulders tense. Dad sucks in his breath and stares at me.

I don't know what I expected, but it wasn't this reaction. "What?" I ask.

"Go on, Kristi. What's your question?" Dad says. He and Mom are looking at me as if I'd asked nothing more threatening than what they want for dessert. What did I just see? It's no longer there. Did I imagine it?

I clear my throat and speak up. "One of the doctors in the hospital thought I was visiting my grandfather."

"Your grandfather?" Mom asks. "What gave the doctor that idea?"

I shrug. "Well, because Mr. Merson had been asking for me. I told the doctor Mr. Merson was *not* my grandfather. I was right, wasn't I?"

Mom's eyes widen with amazement, and Dad looks puzzled.

"Of course you're right. You know Mr. Merson isn't related to us," Mom says.

And Dad adds, "That's a peculiar question, Kristi. I don't know why you'd ask it."

"We've never even met the man," Mom says.

"I'm not adopted," I say. It's a statement, not a question.

"Oh, good heavens," Mom says. "Of course you're not. Don't you think we would have told you?" Impatiently she pushes her chair back from the table and begins to rise, but Dad rests a hand on her arm. He chuckles, surprising both of us.

"Nearly every kid wonders at some time or another if he's been adopted," he says. "I did. You probably did too, Callie. I remember taking a good long look at my parents, seeing all their flaws and thinking there was no way in the world I could have the same genes."

Mom's shoulders drop as she relaxes. She smiles back at Dad. "I was ten," she says. "I was furious with my mother because she wouldn't let me do something I badly wanted to do. I don't even remember now what it was. But I do remember how sure I was that I'd been mixed up with another baby in the hospital and had gone home with the wrong parents."

"I was twelve," he tells her. "We were a lot younger than Kristi is."

They both grin at me. "Clearly, a case of arrested development," Dad says.

"Very funny," I tell them. But I get busy and clear the table, glad that Mom's no longer upset with me about what I said. I shouldn't have asked such a weird question.

———— // ————

I know that when I was born Mom began keeping a scrapbook with lots of photos of me and records of how much I weighed and how tall I grew—all the stuff mothers think is important. She kept it up for years and years. The scrapbook is filled with special school papers and greeting cards I made for Mom and Dad on holidays. I began adding to it myself about the time I started high school.

After the kitchen has been cleaned, I go upstairs to my room and pull down the scrapbook from my closet shelf. On the third page is an envelope with my birth certificate inside. I take out the certificate and study the information on it.

I was born at Houston's Women's Center. Mom was thirty-six when I was born, and Dad was forty-five. The attending physician was Dr. Alonzo Salinas. He's not Mom's doctor now, but I recognize his name. Whenever there's a news story about some new advance in women's health care, the TV reporters interview him. He seems to be a local authority on the subject of women's health.

I wasn't surprised at the ages of my parents when I was born. I knew that Dad was nine years older than Mom and that Mom had been working as a sales clerk when they met. After they'd married he tried to encourage Mom to go back to college and get a degree in accounting. It took a few years, but she finally agreed. Her grades were so good that she made the honors program. She's sometimes talked about the good friends she made in the program and the projects they worked on to raise funds for speakers for events in the honors program. Then, near the end of her senior year, Mom found she was expecting me.

Once, when she'd been reminiscing about it, I shrugged and said, "I must have been bad timing."

Mom laughed and hugged me. "Not at all. Your father and I had tried to have a child for six years.

You've heard of biological clocks? Well, we got a late start and were running out of time. I was afraid we'd never be able to have a child. So we were both ecstatic when we discovered that I was pregnant."

"You never had another child. Just me."

Mom gave me an odd look. Then she said in a quiet voice, "It's not that we didn't want another child. We just couldn't. We considered ourselves very lucky to have had *you!*"

I fold the birth certificate and tuck it back into the envelope. Mom and Dad are my birth parents. There's no doubt about it. There's even a signature on the certificate from the attending doctor at my birth. I trust my parents completely, so what am I trying to find? What am I hoping to prove?

I'm not going to wait until Sunday to visit Mr. Merson. He asked me to come back, so tomorrow I will.

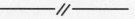

During art club Ms. Montero stops by my desk. "Did you ever call New York and find out from the Museum of Modern Art about the Frank Kupka painting?" she asks.

"They said it wasn't on display right now. But they didn't tell me where it was. The woman I talked to acted suspicious of me." I sigh. "I don't know how to find out if I saw the real painting or not. Actually, I need to know."

"I can help," she says. "I know the person to talk to."

"Thanks," I answer. "That's very nice of you."

She smiles, then points out a spot where a little shading will add a third dimension to my work.

While I have her to myself I ask, "Have you ever been to the Royal Heritage Gallery of Art?"

"Yes," she answers.

I wait for her to go on, but she doesn't, so I ask, "What do you think of it?"

"I don't know much about it, and I've only been there twice," Ms. Montero says.

"Well?" I prod, repeating, "What do you think of it?"

She shrugs, then says, "I think their prices are too high. They do carry some marvelous pieces. Once in a while they handle truly valuable paintings. I remember reading about their sale of a John Constable, and last year they were agents in the purchase of a Camille Pissarro."

"Wow! I'm impressed."

"But they aren't consistent. They occasionally feature what I'd call second-rate artists at first-rate prices." She smiles at me teasingly. "Are you thinking of buying something by one of the old masters?"

"Not yet," I answer, and smile in return. "I'm asking because I met the owner of the gallery."

"Alanna Chase," Ms. Montero says.

"Right."

I wait for Ms. Montero to continue, but she doesn't. "Keep up the good work," she tells me, and moves on to take a look at Jonathan's sketchpad.

Jonathan. Wonderful, handsome Jonathan, who invited me to go with him to the Museum of Fine Arts tomorrow evening. Jonathan makes me completely forget Alanna Chase. I sneak a look from the corners of my eyes and admire the way his profile is backlighted by the sun-soaked windows. I pull out my notebook and make a quick sketch of Jonathan.

At our lockers Lindy reminds me that I promised to go to the office of Child Advocates with her. "Tomorrow after school," she says. "I've got an appointment. Okay?"

"Sure," I tell her. Tomorrow's too far away to think about. My mind is on my upcoming visit with Douglas Merson.

————//————

At the door of Riverview Hospital's room 655, a tall, muscular guy with a thick, hairy neck rises from a wooden chair, blocking my way. For a moment all I can see is his orange-brown checked suit and mustard yellow tie. He's got the right outfit for a bodyguard. That outfit would scare away anyone.

"I'm Kristi Evans," I tell him. "Dr. Lynd said it was all right for me to visit Mr. Merson. He said he'd tell you."

"Go on in," the bodyguard answers. His eyes are bored as he looks away from me, searching the hall. I get the feeling that he quickly loses interest in anyone who doesn't seem to be a threat.

I stop in the open doorway. "What's *your* name?" I ask.

"Gurtz," he says.

"Gurtz? That's all . . . Gurtz?"

"Gurtz," he repeats.

"Thanks, Gurtz," I answer. First name? Last

109

name? What difference does it make? If I had a bodyguard, I'd hate to have someone like Gurtz hanging around.

Gurtz resumes his position in the hallway, and I close the door.

Mr. Merson is propped up in bed. He watches me walk toward him. I can see the pleasure in his eyes.

"You're sitting up. That's great," I tell him. "You'll be going home soon."

He picks up a pad of paper and a pencil. He writes "tomorrow" and holds it up so I can see it.

"So soon? But won't you need a nurse? Someone to change your bandages and take care of you?"

Quickly Mr. Merson writes, "I'll have a private nurse."

"Oh, of course," I say. I should have known. Mr. Merson probably has enough money to hire a whole medical staff.

He motions toward the armchair next to his bed, so I sit down. On the small table next to me is a framed photograph of a guy who looks like he's a senior in high school. He's thin, with pale blond hair, and there's just a touch of a smile on his lips.

Mr. Merson writes, "My son, Roger. He was eighteen at the time. It's the last photograph I have of him."

"I'm sorry about Roger," I say.

He nods. For a few moments he stares down at his hands. Then he turns to a new page in his notepad and writes, "Roger had great promise. He was studying at the University of Houston in the honors program. He would have made a fine architect."

"When did Roger die?"

"Sixteen years ago, while he was still a student."

"I'm sorry." I don't know what else to say, so I change the subject. "You were going to answer some questions for me, before we were interrupted by Sergeant Nims," I tell him. "Will you answer the questions now?"

"You first," he writes.

"I *was* first," I complain. "You were supposed to be next."

"You didn't finish. Tell me about yourself. Tell me what you like to do. Tell me about your artwork."

"You know something about my art—about the awards I won at school."

Mr. Merson waits patiently, so I find myself babbling on. I tell him that I love serious art, but I also love to sketch, and sometimes my sketches become cartoons.

He's actually listening, soaking up every word I say, so I go on. I talk to Mr. Merson as if he's an old friend. I tell him about wanting to go to the summer art school and major in art when I'm in college, then confide that my parents are against it. I tell him what Ms. Montero said that gave me hope that someday I'll do it on my own.

Mr. Merson holds out the pad and pencil to me.

I laugh. "Are you asking me to make a sketch of you?"

He nods, so I set to work and pretty soon I've drawn a comical sketch of a patient in a jumble of bandages, tubes, and bedclothes. His eyes twinkle as though he's part of a huge joke.

When I hand Mr. Merson the pad his eyelids

crinkle, and a chuckle rolls up from the back of his throat. He tears off the page and anchors it on the table with the edge of his son's framed photograph. Then he points a finger at me.

"I get your message. You want me to sit still," I tell him.

I watch with interest as he sets to work. From time to time he looks from me to the paper and back again, and he draws steadily. He takes longer than I did, and I'm eager to see what he's drawn.

Finally he tears off the page and hands it to me. I look at the sketch of my face and shoulders and gasp with surprise. The drawing is not only a perfect likeness, it has a three-dimensional quality. And there's a light behind my eyes that makes me look as though at any moment I'll begin to speak.

"You're a professional artist!" I exclaim. "This is beautiful!" I study the sketch. "The shadows at the side of the face . . . the highlights on the cheekbones . . . Oh! I see how you got that effect. But the quality of making the sketch come alive . . . Will you show me how to do that?"

"Yes. Later," he writes. "You have the talent, so there is a great deal I hope you will learn."

"Oh." Embarrassed, I try to explain. "I won't be able to take art lessons for a few years."

"You will if you have a benefactor."

It takes a moment for what he has written to sink in. "I don't understand. Do you mean *you?*" I blurt out. "Oh, no. I mean, thank you very much, but I couldn't."

"All through history artists have had benefactors."

112

I'm overwhelmed at what he is offering but confused about how to handle it. I don't want to seem rude, but there's no way I can accept his financial help. Flustered, I change the subject. "May I keep this?" I hold the sketch protectively to my chest as though I'm afraid someone will take it away.

"It's yours," he writes.

I lean back in the armchair and smile at him. "Now I know one thing about you—that you're a very talented artist—but I want to know more. It's your turn. Tell me who you are. And tell me why you've kept a file about me."

He writes slowly and holds up the pad. "Later. I'm tired."

I can't tell him what I'd like to—that he's unfair and that he's avoiding my questions. He's recovering from serious injuries, and he probably tires very easily.

As I get to my feet he writes, "Bring your parents to my home on Sunday."

My parents. I've forgotten them and the visit they've planned.

"I will," I answer. "And thank you for the beautiful drawing."

He nods, then leans back against the pillow. He looks exhausted, and I feel guilty for thinking he was trying to escape from answering my questions.

"Goodbye, Gurtz," I say as I pass the hulk in the hallway.

Gurtz grunts in return, which is probably the best he can do.

I should feel pleased with my visit to Mr. Merson. He enjoyed it, and the drawing was a wonder-

113

ful gift. I still feel uncomfortable about his offer to be my benefactor, but something else bothers me, and I don't know what it is. It's not until I climb into the car and turn on the ignition that the stray uncomfortable thoughts come together with a snap.

Sixteen years ago Roger was in the honors program at the University of Houston. So was my mother.

Why did my mother tell me she didn't know Roger?

CHAPTER ELEVEN

—— // ——

It's a quarter to five when I reach home. I pick up the telephone and stare at it. Maybe everyone in the offices at the University of Houston has gone home by this time. Then again, maybe not. It's worth finding out.

To my surprise I reach the director of the honors program without any trouble.

"Barry Jenkins here," he says.

"Hi," I say. "I need to ask about someone who was at the University of Houston in the honors program a number of years ago."

"I may not be able to help you," Mr. Jenkins answers. "I've been in this job for only three years."

"Oh." Disappointment rises in a lump and clogs

my throat. "Well, this was sixteen years ago. Thank you very—"

"Hey, wait," he says. "You're in luck. I was a student in the honors program at that time, so maybe I can answer your question. So tell me, what's your name and what do you want to know?"

Hope fills my body like helium. I introduce myself. "My mother was in the honors program then. Callie Evans. Do you know her?"

"You bet I do. We were good friends. How is Callie?"

"She's fine, thanks."

"What do you want to know about her that she can't tell you herself?"

"It's not about Mom," I tell him. "It's about someone named Roger Merson."

"Oh, gosh, yeah," he says. "Roger. You know he committed suicide."

"Yes."

"It really got to your mother. He was a badly mixed-up kid—drugs and alcohol—and Callie had taken him under her wing. She did her best to turn his life around. When he died, Callie blamed herself. She thought she hadn't done enough."

In shock I stammer, "Sh-She knew him? She knew Roger Merson?"

"Sure. Except she didn't know him as Roger Merson. None of us did. He'd broken away from his family. I think they lived in California. At least his mother did. There was a lot of anger on Roger's part, especially with his father. Roger refused to use his name. But I found all this out later. At the time we knew him as Chip Blair."

116

"When he died, didn't you learn his real name?"

"No. Chip had mailed a letter to the director of the honors program. He told him who to contact. After the first story about the suicide on the back pages of the newspaper, there wasn't another word. I guess the police must have notified his family, and they took care of everything. We did have a memorial service for Chip. That's all we knew to do."

"When did you all find out that Chip was really Roger?" I ask. I'm still puzzled about Mom's denial.

"As I told you, we didn't," Mr. Jenkins says. "I'm probably one of the few of our group who knows the facts, and that's because I went through the former director's files after I took this job."

"So Mom really doesn't know." I must have spoken my thoughts aloud, because Mr. Jenkins answers me.

"It happened a long time ago. Is there some reason Callie should be told about it now? It might just bring back a lot of unhappiness."

"You're right," I mumble. He's waiting for some kind of explanation, but I don't know what else to say.

"Call me if you need me," he says.

"I will," I answer. "Thank you for your help."

We say goodbye, and I hang up. Telling Mom that she really does have a tie to the Mersons is going to be tough. I can't rush into it. I've got to think it out. What am I going to say? How am I going to put it?

Mom. Guess what I found out.

No! That's awful. I shudder. I've got to come up with a better idea.

117

Mom. I've got something to tell you . . . something sad to tell you.

That might work. I'll start by saying, *Sit down, Mom. I've got something sad to tell you.* I sigh and lean back in my chair. That might prepare her for what she's going to hear.

I'm so busy trying to decide just how to break this news to Mom that I forget all about starting dinner. I don't give it a thought until Mom and Dad walk through the kitchen door.

Mom stops in the middle of the kitchen and stares around the room. "What happened to dinner?" she asks.

"Dinner? Oh, no! I forgot about dinner."

"You forgot to make dinner? Kristi, what's wrong? Something's happened, hasn't it?"

"Mom, sit down," I begin. "I've got something sad to tell you."

"What is it, Kristi?" Mom's voice rises, and she clutches the back of a chair. "It's not your grandma, is it? Oh, please, no! Not your grandma!"

The color in Mom's face drains to a sickly gray. Dad grabs her and helps lower her into the chair.

I panic and shout, "It's not Grandma. Grandma's fine. Mom, I found out today that your friend Chip Blair wasn't really Chip Blair. I mean, that wasn't his name. He had told everybody that was his name because he'd made a break with his family. His name was really Roger Merson."

Some color has come back into Mom's face, but she stares at me with blank eyes. Her lips are parted. Her mouth hangs slightly open.

118

It's taking Dad too a few moments to figure out what I'm talking about.

"Mom . . . Dad . . . I tried to figure out a way to tell you without getting you upset. I even practiced what I'd say. But I did it all wrong. I'm so sorry."

Mom gives a huge sigh and slumps in her chair. "Chip Blair was really Roger Merson? Are you sure? How did you find out, Kristi?"

"I talked to the director of the honors program at the University of Houston. His name is Barry Jenkins."

Mom perks up at this. "Barry is director now? Good for him."

"I wish I'd asked him to tell you about Roger. He would have done a better job."

Mom slowly gets up and wraps her arms around me. "Honey, you did your best. I jumped to conclusions, that's all. I made it more difficult for you."

Dad puts an arm around Mom's shoulders. Pretty soon we're into a three-way hug. "Your mother tried to get Chip into rehab," Dad says, "and she did. During his senior year he was completely drug free. Callie helped Chip study so he wouldn't flunk out. She tried to get him to make peace with his family. She never gave up."

"The morning they found Chip's body, someone told us. I don't even remember now who it was," Mom says. "I do remember how devastated I felt. I'd thought I'd been helping Chip, and I hadn't."

"You can't blame yourself," Dad and I say, practically together.

119

"Chip was as mixed up as anyone could get," Dad says.

Mom goes on. "Chip and I became friendly. It was nice for me, since college was a big adjustment from working. He needed a friend too. He had terrible arguments with his father, who was a dominating, difficult person. The man wanted to control Chip's life. Chip's father had decided he should be an architect. He had arranged for the right contacts for Chip so as soon as he had his degree he'd have the perfect job. He'd even handpicked a wife for Chip and talked to him about how much he wanted an heir.

"Chip needed someone to talk to. He said he loved his father, yet at the same time he hated him. He went back and forth between trying to please him and defying him. I never met Chip's father. I didn't know he was . . ."

Mom breaks off. We all stare at each other. "Douglas Merson," Mom says.

She backs toward the chair and sits down again. "Is all this mysterious behavior on Mr. Merson's part some kind of revenge? Does the man blame me for what happened to his son?"

"It couldn't be that," I tell her, although I've got chills up and down my backbone. I don't think I've ever felt so confused. "Mr. Merson has been very nice to me, Mom."

I grab my bag and pull out the sheet of paper with the drawing on it. I show it to them and say, "He drew this of me today."

Mom takes a closer look. "It looks just like you! Kristi, he's a real artist. Did you know this?"

"I just found out this afternoon," I answer.

"He's a professional artist, all right," Dad says. He takes another look at the sketch, then places it carefully on the table. He turns and looks at me. "Now let's get down to basic facts, Kristi. How did you happen to call the director of the honors program? What information did you have that led you to do that?"

That's the way Dad's mind works. Facts. X equals whatever and proves to be correct. Everything nice and tidy and mathematical. Well, maybe that's what's needed right now—a good mathematical mind.

"Mr. Merson showed me a photograph of his son, taken while he was in high school," I answer. "He told me—"

"Told you?" Mom interrupts. "He can speak?"

"*Wrote*, not told. On a pad of paper. He wrote that his son was in the honors program at the University of Houston sixteen years ago. Later I remembered that you were there at the same time, Mom. But you said you didn't know Roger Merson, so I called, not even thinking anyone was there. I just needed to find out why."

Mom and Dad look at each other. Then Mom turns back to me and says, "You went to the hospital to see Mr. Merson today."

"Yes."

"After what we said?"

"You didn't actually tell me I couldn't."

Dad's gaze is like a drill. "Kristi, is there anything you haven't told us? Anything we should know about?"

121

"No," I say. "Except that Mr. Merson has a body-guard now. His name is Gurtz. And the hospital is letting him go home tomorrow. And he invited us to come and see him in his home on Sunday afternoon."

Mom puts her head in her hands and groans. "I don't want to see him. Not Sunday. Not ever."

Dad rests one hand on her shoulder. With the other he smoothes back her hair. "You don't have to, Callie. I'll go alone. At least one of us should talk to him. We need to find out why Mr. Merson has such a strange interest in Kristi."

Mom sits back and looks up at Dad. "You're not going by yourself," she says. "I'm going with you."

"I'm going too," I tell them. "I'm just as eager to know the answer as you are."

"Kristi, I don't want you to go with us Sunday," Mom says. "I don't want you to have anything more to do with Douglas Merson."

I'm so shocked I gasp for breath. "But I have to go, Mom! Detective Balker said we all should go. And Mr. Merson invited me to come and bring my parents. *Me*, Mom. He won't like it if I'm not there. Maybe he won't tell you anything."

Dad says quietly, "Kristi may be right, Callie. Maybe she should go. I don't think there will be a problem. We'll be with her."

It's hard to breathe as I wait for Mom's answer. Finally she says, "All right. On Sunday. But, Kristi, no more trips alone to visit Mr. Merson. Understand?"

Relieved, I nod. "I understand."

Dad sighs, and I say, "Please don't let this make you unhappy."

"I'm not unhappy," Dad says. "I'm hungry. Let's put this aside for now and run over to Luby's Cafeteria for something to eat."

Mom pulls herself together and gets to her feet. "Give me a couple of minutes to get ready."

While I'm waiting I start thinking. For the first time it occurs to me that on Sunday we'll be inside Mr. Merson's home. I can stand in front of Kupka's painting and soak in the colors. Maybe Mr. Merson has other paintings. Mr. Merson is an artist. I wonder if any of his own work is on display in his house. I wonder what he paints. On Sunday I may find out.

For just an instant I see myself as a successful artist in an elegant home. It would take years of practice and study and . . . lessons. And some way to pay for them. Or someone. A benefactor.

Absolutely not. No way. I push the tempting offer from my mind. I don't even know who Douglas Merson is.

———— // ————

On Friday afternoon I drive Lindy downtown to the Child Advocates offices on Main Street. The receptionist greets us pleasantly and picks up the phone to notify someone that Lindy is there for her appointment.

"You'll be talking with Ms. Taylor, one of our volunteers. She'll be with you in just a few minutes," the receptionist tells Lindy. She gestures

123

toward a grouping of upholstered chairs. "You can wait over there."

"Thanks," Lindy says.

As we sit down, two women stroll into the reception room from the hallway. "I know another case even more heartbreaking than the one you're working on," one woman tells the other one. "Maybe you read about it or saw it on the news last year."

She describes the case of a test-tube baby wanted and fought over by the egg donor, the sperm donor, and the surrogate mother. "That poor little girl is two now—no time to be taken from the woman she's always known as mother. She badly needs an advocate," the woman says.

"Don't they all! I'm working with two children from a family with substance abuse, and those sweet babies need all the help they can get." The other woman looks at her watch. "I have to get to a meeting over near the Galleria. I'll see you on Wednesday."

The receptionist answers her phone, then leaves her desk. She says to us, "Come with me, girls. I'll take you to Ms. Taylor's office."

By the time Lindy and I leave the offices, she's clutching a stack of pamphlets and flyers. We've learned that volunteers are trained to represent in court children from abusive homes who are temporarily in foster care. But volunteers also help children feel secure, taking them to the park, giving them birthday parties, and just showing they care.

As Lindy and I climb into the car, she settles into the seat with a sigh. "Everything we heard makes me really appreciate my own parents."

"That's exactly the way I feel," I answer.

We ride in silence. My own mom and dad don't always see things the way I do. They can't begin to understand how much I want to study to become an artist. And yet right now, more than ever before in my life, I feel close to them. I'm awfully glad I've got them.

CHAPTER TWELVE

———— // ————

Mom and Dad are on hand when Jonathan comes to pick me up Friday evening. They chat with him for a few minutes, both of them wearing extra-pleasant faces as they ask horrible questions: "Do you have a college in mind yet?" and "Do you know what you want to major in?"

I know Jonathan probably thinks he's being grilled. I feel bad that he's suffering.

But then I wonder, What should parents talk about when they meet their daughter's dates? Rising prices? Stock quotations? Problems with an aging garbage disposal? Parents have nothing at all in common with the guys who ask out their daughters. The best thing to do is keep the conversations as short as possible.

I take Jonathan's arm. "We've got to hurry," I tell Mom and Dad. "We're supposed to be at the museum by seven-thirty."

We say goodbye all around. Jonathan doesn't seem to mind when Mom adds, "Drive carefully."

As we get into his car Jonathan says, "Your parents are nice."

"Thanks," I answer.

Jonathan begins to relax, and we talk. I find out that Jonathan's on his neighborhood tennis team and coaches the little kids' swim team. He's taking art at his mother's insistence.

"My fifth-grade teacher told her I showed promise," he says, "so I've been dragged around to art classes ever since." He makes a face. "My mom's grandmother painted landscapes. I guess her stuff was okay. My mom's always bragging about it. She thinks I inherited the family talent."

"My grandmother keeps telling me I draw like her brother," I say. "My parents don't brag about art things!"

"Are you going to take that summer art course?" he asks.

I shake my head. "Don't even ask. It makes me too unhappy. My parents think art lessons are a waste of money."

"Trade you parents," Jonathan says. He smiles at me.

"It's a deal," I tell him. I'm warm and happy. I like the low music of Jonathan's voice.

We capture one of the last parking places in the lot across the street from the museum. Right on time we meet Ms. Montero and some of the kids in

127

our class. There's a line, but it moves pretty fast. Before long we're surrounded by French paintings from the eighteenth century. Ms. Montero points out details and fills in history and makes it all interesting to me.

I can tell, though, that Jonathan doesn't care that much.

As we fall behind the group in the last room of the exhibition, Jonathan leans close to me and murmurs in my ear, "Not much longer and we'll be out of here."

"You don't like the exhibition?"

"No," he says. "Do you?"

"It's not my favorite," I answer. "Most of the paintings are too elaborate and busy. Except for a few. I did like the one with the mother and daughters called *Saying Grace*."

Jonathan shrugs, and I tease him, "Think of the extra credit we get for this trip. That's why you came, isn't it?"

"No," he says. "You were the first one to raise your hand, so I raised mine. I came because of you."

My heart beats loudly in my ears. Why doesn't everyone in the room turn to see where the drumbeats are coming from?

Jonathan doesn't seem to hear them. And he doesn't realize that my brain has frozen, my mouth won't open, and my legs—which I'm counting on to hold me up—have melted away.

"When we get through here, want to go to Marble Slab and get some ice cream?" Jonathan asks.

"Sure," I hear myself saying, and realize with sur-

prise that everything still works. Wonderful, handsome, superterrific Jonathan. He came to an art
exhibition just because of me.

"I always get amaretto cream with chunks of milk
chocolate folded in," he says.

"Make that two," I tell him.

"Okay. What will *you* have?" he asks.

We keep up the easy banter until after we go and
get our cones and have to lick the dripping ice
cream as fast as we can before it melts. We sit at a
tiny metal table outside, facing the parking lot on
Memorial, slowly enjoying what's left of our cones.

A family that has tromped across the lot enters
the store, leaving us blissfully alone. Jonathan leans
down and kisses me lightly on the lips.

His kiss is cold and sticky and tastes of almond. I
lift my chin and kiss him back.

"Want to go to a movie tomorrow night?" he
asks.

"Oh, yes," I answer.

"Wait a minute. I forgot about my report," Jonathan says. "Make that Sunday afternoon. Instead of
a movie, we could drive to the beach."

"I can't Sunday." I don't know why, but I'm re-
luctant to tell Jonathan about Mr. Merson, so I just
say, "Mom and Dad and I have to visit a man who's
just out of the hospital. We said we'd come on Sunday afternoon. I have to be there."

"I wish I could get out of what I have to do
tomorrow night," Jonathan says. "I have to write a
report on test-tube babies for my social problems
class. We're working on community resources or

something. I've got to interview a doctor, and he said he couldn't see me until Saturday."

"Lindy Baker's in your class," I tell him. "I went with her to talk to someone at Child Advocates. She's doing her report on them." I tell him a little about what the volunteers do and about the conversation we overheard. "I feel so sorry for that child they were talking about. She was a test-tube baby."

Jonathan says, "The question concerning my topic, test-tube babies, is, 'These people want a child. What can we do to help them?' Nobody asks the next question, 'How is what we do going to affect the child?' "

"There aren't many test-tube babies, are there?" I ask. "Isn't that something they've just begun to experiment with?"

"No. It's been going on for years. They don't even really say 'test-tube' anymore. I've got an appointment with one of the doctors who specialized in fertility problems. He helped pioneer in vitro insemination—a Dr. Alonzo Salinas. He's retired now, but he said he'd be glad to talk to me. He's in some kind of golf tournament this weekend, so the only time he could see me is Saturday evening."

Dr. Alonzo Salinas. My brain tries to absorb what I've just heard, but it's hard to think. I feel the last inch of cone shatter in my hand, and ice cream oozes between my fingers.

When I can finally speak, my voice trembles. "Jonathan," I beg, "please, could I go with you?"

He pops the end of his cone into his mouth,

130

munches, gulps, then smiles. He hasn't noticed a thing, and I'm glad. I don't want to explain. "It's real nice of you to offer to keep me company, Kristi," he says. "You should get a grade, since you've worked with Lindy and me! Are you sure you want to go?"

I take a deep breath. "I'm very sure."

———— // ————

Dr. Salinas lives in a large, two-story dark red brick home on a street off North Boulevard, near the Medical Center. The gnarled oaks that line the streets in this neighborhood are so old and so huge that their branches form an extended tunnel of shade.

Jonathan parks in front of the doctor's house, and I follow him up the walk to the front porch.

An elderly woman with a crown of white curly hair opens the door and smiles at us. Jonathan introduces us, and the woman ushers us into what she calls "the parlor."

It's a long, elegant room with a marble fireplace at one end and dark red velvet drapes at the windows. The furniture is mahogany, with claw feet. I bet myself that all the pieces are real antiques, not reproductions.

Mrs. Salinas seats us on an ornate love seat, then sits opposite us. "The doctor will be down in a few minutes," she says. "He did well at the golf tournament, so he's in a very chipper mood."

131

I'm glad he's feeling happy. Maybe he'll answer the questions I hope I'll be able to ask him.

Mrs. Salinas chats on, and Jonathan answers her. But my attention is caught by the painting that hangs on the wall behind her. It's a cluster of farm-houses among tangled branches of trees. The roofs of the houses are red, and the roofs and walls gleam warmly in the sunlight. I recognize the painting.

"Camille Pissarro," I say.

Mrs. Salinas smiles at me. "That's right. I trea-sure that painting. It brings back so many happy memories of our trips to France."

"It's a beautiful reproduction," I tell her.

"Oh, it's not a reproduction, dear. It's an origi-nal," Mrs. Salinas tells me, pride in her voice. "It was a birthday gift last year from the doctor."

Before I can think, I blurt out, "I thought *Red Roofs* was owned by a museum in Paris."

"One of them is," Mrs. Salinas says. "We were told that Pissarro apparently painted a number of versions of *Red Roofs*. According to the dealer, this painting was found in an attic where it had been hidden for years. We were so fortunate to obtain it."

"Yes, you were," I murmur. "Did your husband buy the painting in Paris?"

"No," she answers. "It's so nice that you know about art." She smiles and continues, "The trans-action was made through a local gallery, people who've been well established for years. We've bought paintings through them before, and so have our friends. You may have heard of the Royal Heri-tage Gallery of Art."

132

This must be the Pissarro painting Ms. Montero referred to when I asked her about Ms. Chase and her gallery. I relax and feast my eyes on the light and shadow and warm colors in the painting. It's beautiful.

Dr. Salinas strides into the room. The fragrance of soap follows him, and his sparse hair is still damp from his shower. He's slightly bent, and the knuckles on his hands are so large and gnarled I'm reminded of the knobs on the crepe myrtle trees outside his front door. Jonathan and I jump to our feet, and Jonathan goes through the introductions again.

"Would you young people like a Coke or some iced tea?" Mrs. Salinas asks.

Together we answer, "No, thank you." I can't imagine swallowing anything, and I know Jonathan is as scared as I am because as we drove here he told me so.

I sit quietly while Jonathan opens his notebook and begins to ask questions. I listen intently and hear about the mistakes that were made in early in vitro insemination, the failures, and finally the successes as eggs were retrieved, inseminated, then transferred to the uterus, where fertilization could take place.

Jonathan has given a lot of thought to his questions. He goes into opposition to the project; the fate of the living cells that are impregnated, then discarded; and the ethics involved.

Finally he checks over his notes, closes his notebook, and says, "I think that's about it."

"Well, then—" Dr. Salinas begins.

"May I ask a question?" I interrupt. My words are breathy, I'm so eager for answers.

Dr. Salinas and Jonathan turn to look at me.

Before either can respond, I hurry to say, "Who were your sperm donors? Where did they come from?"

Jonathan nods with approval and opens his notebook again. It's a good question and one he didn't think to ask.

"With my work here in Houston the donors were students at the university—bright young men in good health. Their names were kept confidential, of course," the doctor tells me.

"Even the women whose eggs were fertilized didn't know who the donors were?"

"They were not told."

"What about in a court of law? Where someone needs to know the name of the donor? Can't they find out?"

Dr. Salinas shakes his head. "The records are sealed."

I can't give up. I approach the doctor in a different way. "Then even though the father of the child was a donor, the woman's husband's name would be on the birth certificate. Is that right?"

"Yes. That's right. That is the law."

I'm so scared, I grip my fingers together to keep them from shaking. "Did all your patients have fertility problems?"

"Most of them."

"And they all agreed to participate in creating test-tube babies?"

"By no means," Dr. Salinas says. "We treated

many women—and sometimes their husbands—
with medication or surgery."

"If I give you the name of one of your patients,
would you remember—"

Dr. Salinas leans forward as he interrupts me.
"You should know, young lady, that with any doctor a patient's records are completely confidential
and not open to any other party. I can't discuss a
patient with you."

With some difficulty he pushes himself to his
feet. Jonathan and I scramble to stand.

"Thanks for letting us come," Jonathan says.

In a small voice I manage to thank him too.

"You're welcome," Dr. Salinas says to Jonathan.
"Good luck with your report."

As we walk to the car, I dart quick looks at Jonathan. I wonder if he's angry at me.

But as we settle into the car and he turns on the
ignition, he says, "That was a good question about
who the donors were. Thanks for asking it. And I
hadn't thought about asking if the in vitro work
took up all his time. It was interesting to know that
he had other patients and other methods of treating
infertility."

"I went too far," I say. "I shouldn't have asked
about a particular patient. I didn't mean to upset
him."

"It's okay, Kristi," Jonathan says. "He wasn't that
upset. I know how you feel about that little kid you
told me about. The story got to you. It bothers me,
too."

He reaches over to take my hand and squeezes it.
I don't try to tell him his assumption is wrong. "I'm

135

glad you came," he says. "It's still early. Want to get pizza and hear some music?"

"I'd love to," I tell him.

"Now that the interview's over, I can relax," Jonathan says. "It's a good feeling to know that I got answers to all my questions."

I desperately wish I could say the same thing.

CHAPTER THIRTEEN

—— // ——

Getting ready to visit Douglas Merson is a pain, and it's Mom who's making it so difficult.

"Kristi, you aren't going to wear jeans!"

"Why not, Mom? I wore them the last time I went to visit Mr. Merson in the hospital."

Mom groans. "This visit is different. We're going to his house. Wear what you wore this morning to church. Remember, it's Sunday."

"What does Sunday have to do with wearing jeans?" I ask.

"Kristi!" I can tell from Mom's voice that there's no use arguing. "Put on a dress. And stockings. And your good shoes. And please, do something with your hair. Get it out of your eyes."

Mom doesn't know what Mr. Merson will tell us.

A part of me wants to comfort her. I want to hug her and say, "Hey, look, whatever reason he gives us for keeping that folder about me doesn't matter."

But it *does* matter because I think I already know his reason. And I'm scared too.

I back off from Mom and run upstairs to change. I've always believed everything Mom and Dad ever told me. I've never questioned them because I've trusted them. Are things different now? It shakes me.

I lean toward the bathroom mirror, my hairbrush in my hand, then stop and stare hard at my reflection. "Who are you?" I whisper.

The doorbell jangles, and I jump.

Mom yells up the stairs, "Kristi!" So I smooth back my hair, fasten it with a clip, and hurry down the stairs.

Detective Balker smiles up at me from the foot of the stairs. I'm surprised to see him. "We're getting ready to visit Mr. Merson," I tell him.

"I know," he says. "I just came by to make sure the meeting was still on." As he takes a step toward the door he says to Mom, "I'll meet you folks over there. You can ask him whatever questions you want, but we'll keep the visit short."

"Of course," Mom says. She looks the way she did when she had the flu. She's put color on her cheeks, but she's so pale underneath that the two pink ovals stand out, looking weird.

"Does it have to be a short visit?" I ask Balker. "Mr. Merson has a fabulous painting in his entry hall. He's an artist himself. I'd love to see his work."

138

"Kristi!" Mom explodes. "Be reasonable! This is not a social call. Mr. Merson is not a friend. We're not hoping to have a pleasant chat with him."

Her anger startles me.

"See you there," Balker says, and quickly leaves the house.

I get a tissue from the pop-up box in the guest bathroom. "Hold still," I tell Mom, and I blend in the stark edges of color on her cheeks.

Mom glances into the mirror in the entry hall. "Thanks, honey," she says. Her eyes fill with tears.

Dad claps a hand on Mom's shoulder. "Everything's going to be all right," he tells her. "Merson can't hurt Kristi."

"He can't?" Mom says. "Look what he did to his son."

"Mr. Merson loved his son!" I'm surprised at myself for strongly defending a man I don't even know.

Mom takes the tissue from me and wipes her eyes. "If a parent really loves a child, he nurtures him. He doesn't try to control him." Her words seem to bounce off the walls and into our private thoughts.

I want to say, *How about not allowing the child to major in art, when that's what she wants most in the world to study?* But I don't. I can tell from Mom's and Dad's expressions that they've thought of that.

Finally Dad clears his throat and asks, "Are you both ready to leave? We don't want to keep Detective Balker waiting."

Mom takes a deep breath and throws back her shoulders. "We're coming," she says firmly.

I silently follow my parents out to the car.

On the way to Merson's house we don't talk. There doesn't seem to be anything to say. But as we near Chimney Rock I give Dad directions on how to reach Merson's house on Buffalo Bayou Lane.

As we pull into the drive behind Balker's car, he climbs out and waits for us to join him. The four of us walk slowly to the front porch. Mom grips Dad's arm tightly.

Mom's nervousness is contagious. I begin to fear whatever it is Mr. Merson is going to tell us.

Frederick opens the door. Gurtz looms behind him. I feel intimidated. I let Balker do all the talking.

We're ushered into the entry hall, and I find myself face-to-face with the Kupka painting. The vibrant bands of color reach out to me. They wipe every other thought from my mind. "See, Mom? Look, Dad. This is Frank Kupka's portrait of his wife." I check the bottom of the canvas. There, in neat script, is the signature: *František Kupka.*

Mom gives the painting only a quick glance, but Dad studies it, frowning. "I don't get it," he says in a low voice. "You can hardly see the woman's face. Why did the artist slap those strips of color all over her? Couldn't he have had her sit in a chair? Maybe with some flowers in a vase next to her? I bet she wasn't too happy with this portrait."

Discouraged, I don't even try to answer.

A nurse, wearing a tidy white uniform, comes into the hall and smiles at us. "I'm Connie Babson," she tells us. Ms. Babson is short and plump and middle-aged and looks as if she laughs easily. If I had to be taken care of, I'd like a nurse like her.

"You're the first guests Mr. Merson has had," she says. She leans toward Mom, as though she's confiding in her. "We'll keep our visit short because he tires easily."

We're led into a large living area with stark white walls, white upholstery, a white marble fireplace, and even a white carpet. I suck in my breath. We've been thrown into a stage setting in which the rows of paintings on the walls are the stars. Muted colors, bright colors, textures both soft, like old, faded silk, and bold, with thick, rough brush strokes. Soothing landscapes, imposing portraits, and impressions so wild they shout.

On the far side are windows that look out onto a roofed patio. A sparkling blue swimming pool lies just beyond.

Mom and Dad are being introduced by Sergeant Balker. I forcibly rip myself from this world of beauty and say hello to Mr. Merson.

He's propped up with pillows on a large sofa and covered with a light wool blanket. In his hands he holds a pad of paper and a pencil. He nods at each of us in turn, his eyes showing a smile as they meet mine. I notice that he studies Mom for a long time.

"Please be seated," Ms. Babson tells us.

Four chairs have been arranged so that they're facing the sofa, and we sit down. Ms. Babson hovers over Mr. Merson behind the sofa, and Gurtz stands at the door, his arms folded across his chest.

I lean toward Mr. Merson, overcome by the art that surrounds us. "I wish you could tell me about each of your paintings," I say. "Are some of them your own work?"

141

He nods and points to four canvases, one of which I would have guessed was a Chagall, with its strange cow heads and scrap of a rural village. Then he writes, "The real thing. Turner," and points to a subdued landscape. And "Monet," then points to a scene of water lilies.

Wow! This is like living in a museum.

"Where do you paint?" I ask. "Is your studio in your house?"

Mom grips my arm. "That's enough, Kristi," she says, although she doesn't look at me. She looks directly at Mr. Merson. "Mr. Merson knows why we're here."

He writes something and holds up the pad so we can read it. "Kristi has been kind to me. She's a fine young woman. I know you are very proud of her."

"Well, yes. Of course we are proud of her," Mom says. She twists her fingers together.

"Kristi realizes how important art is in my life," Mr. Merson writes. "Please forgive her for indulging me."

Mom squirms as though she doesn't know what to say next. I think she must have worked out a plan before we came, but Mr. Merson just wiped it out.

Dad steps in. "Mr. Merson, we need to know why you have held this long-term interest in our daughter."

Mr. Merson holds up a hand, the way a traffic cop would signal drivers to stop. For a few seconds he writes. Then he holds up the pad. "Is Kristi receiving the instruction she needs?"

Dad and Mom look at each other in surprise. "She's in high school—Carter High," Dad answers.

"Instruction in art?" Mr. Merson writes.

"She belongs to an art club that meets after school," Mom says. Impatience creeps into her voice.

Mr. Merson writes, "It's not enough. She has talent that needs to be directed."

Mom's temper begins to rise. "*We're* her parents. We'll be the judge of that."

Just then Frederick comes into the room. He walks carefully, balancing a tray that holds four glasses of iced tea, sprigged with mint. As he pauses before each of us we say, "No, thank you."

The tea looks good, and I'd really like to have some, but what if I spilled even a drop on the gorgeous white carpeting? It's a lot safer to leave the tea in Frederick's hands. I think my parents probably feel the same.

Mom is ready to go back into battle, but Mr. Merson hands Ms. Babson a note. She reads it, walks to the far end of the sofa, and picks up a small, framed photograph—the one I saw in the hospital. She carries the photo to Mom.

"Oh! It's Chip," Mom says. I can hear the tears in her voice.

I glance at Mr. Merson, and he's studying Mom, his gaze so intent, it's as if he's trying to peer inside her head.

Mom looks up from the photograph. "I'm sorry about your son, Mr. Merson," she says. "Chip's death was painful to all of us in the honors program. We all felt close to each other. We celebrated together, and we shared each other's problems."

"Roger was an artist too. He had great promise," Mr. Merson writes.

"I know. Chip . . . that is, *Roger*, shared some of his drawings with me."

Mr. Merson writes another note to Ms. Babson. She hurries over to the end table again and picks up a manila folder. As she hands it to Mom, she takes Roger's photograph, returning it to the table.

Mom opens the folder on her lap, and I lean close to see what it contains. There is a sketch of a laughing young woman, sitting on the rim of a fountain. Her hair is long and hangs down her back. Her hands rest on her bulging abdomen. There's no mistaking who the woman is. At the bottom of the page is a signature: *Roger Merson*.

"Mom!" I exclaim. "That's a great picture of you!"

A tear rolls down Mom's nose, and she wipes it away with the back of one hand. "It was a beautiful, sunny day, and some of us were sitting out by the fountain," she says. "I was so happy because I was expecting *you*, Kristi. I knew Chip was sketching, but he never did show me what he had drawn."

Mr. Merson's eyes seem puzzled, but Mom doesn't notice. She wipes her eyes again and says to him, "Thank you for letting me see this sketch. It brings back happy memories of Ch—Roger. He'd been off drugs for a year. He was working hard on his studies. He was trying to make peace with you.

He had plans. At least we thought . . ." Her voice breaks.

She passes the folder to Dad and folds her hands in her lap. Mom takes a deep breath and says calmly, "Mr. Merson, you know that Drew, Kristi, and I need an answer to our questions. Why have you kept a folder of newspaper clippings about Kristi? Why have you hired people to photograph her during the last sixteen years? What is your reason? Please tell us."

Mr. Merson seems to slip deeply inside himself, like a sea creature hiding in a shell. For a few moments he closes his eyes. Then he opens them and writes, "Later. I'm tired now."

Mom gives a little cry. "That's not fair. We deserve an answer."

She glances to Balker for help, but he shrugs and shakes his head.

Connie Babson takes charge. Smiling, she removes the folder from Mom's hands. In an instant we're all on our feet. Mom, Dad, and Sergeant Balker walk toward the entry hall, but I stop by the sofa and look down on Mr. Merson.

"You're cheating," I say in a low voice. "Why not tell us? You can't put it off forever."

He opens his eyes and looks up at me. "Come back and see me, Kristi," he writes.

"If I do, will you tell me?"

"I'll tell you when it's time."

"Will you let me see your other paintings too?" I ask. "Will you tell me about the Kupka painting in your hall?"

145

He looks surprised, but he writes, "Come back. We need to discuss your future."

At the moment I don't know if I'll return or not. I'm angry, so I don't answer him.

As I turn to walk away, I can see that he's wrestling with problems too.

"Kristi, your parents are waiting for you," Ms. Babson calls from the doorway.

"Okay, I'll come back," I say in a low voice to Mr. Merson.

CHAPTER FOURTEEN

———— // ————

Questions spin through my mind, twisting themselves into a tangled mess because none of them have answers. Mom thought she was helping Chip . . . Roger . . . to turn his life around, but he ended it. Chip hadn't shown the sketch he did of Mom to her. Instead, he signed it *Roger,* and his father has it.

I think about the secret sketches I've drawn of Jonathan. Nobody knows about them but me. Chip might have planned to give the sketch to Mom later, maybe even as a gift when her baby was born. He signed his real name, as any artist would. After Chip's death, his father probably went through his things and packed them. Is that how Mr. Merson got the drawing?

Mom's brooding, and Dad retreats into silence, so I call Lindy and ask if I can come over.

"Sure," she says. "I've been working all day on my report, and I'm ready to relax. I've got this new really great CD we can listen to."

Ten minutes later I'm at Lindy's house. We make brownies and eat some of them still hot from the oven. We listen to music, and I tell her about my Friday-night date with Jonathan and about going for pizza with him on Saturday night. I don't tell her about the visit to Dr. Salinas, though. This is something I need to keep to myself.

But it's fun to talk about Jonathan and what he said and what I said. The questions that have to do with Mr. Merson get tucked away, into a hidden pocket of my mind.

When I get home I quickly kiss Mom and Dad goodnight and run up the stairs to bed.

As I lie in the darkness, warm under my quilt, drifting slowly into sleep, I see Mr. Merson's words: *your future*. An electric jolt of excitement jabs me, and my eyes fly open. *My future as an artist!* It's suddenly so real, I want to reach out and cup my future in my hands and hold it tightly. *My future as an artist.* Mr. Merson wants to give me the future I dream of.

I squeeze my eyes shut and burrow into my pillow. This is no time to wrestle with what this means. I'll think about it tomorrow.

The next morning, as I enter my art appreciation class, Ms. Montero calls me to her desk. "I made that telephone call, Kristi," she says.

At first I'm blank. Then I remember. "Oh. To the Museum of Modern Art in New York?"

"That's right. About the Kupka painting. I was told that *Madame Kupka among Verticals* is with a group of paintings on temporary exhibit in Milwaukee."

Then it hasn't been stolen. I'm puzzled, and I say, "But I saw it yesterday."

"You must have seen a copy. I hope the owner is aware that his painting is only a copy. Of course, it might be a forgery."

"What's the difference between a copy of a painting and a forgery?" I ask.

"A copy is recognized as the work of someone other than the original painter," she answers. "A forgery is a copy that is represented as the original painting itself. In a forgery, there's an intent to deceive."

"But this painting looks so real!"

"A good forgery is hard to detect. Forgers have developed many ways of making their work seem authentic. If it's supposed to be an older painting, it's baked and aged artificially—sometimes under an ultraviolet lamp. Age cracks in the paint can be added by taking the canvas off the stretcher and rubbing it over the edge of a table. Occasionally stolen gallery labels giving numbers and dates of exhibit—faked, of course—are on the back of the canvas. The history and verification of the painting are falsified as well. Some forgers are so skillful they can fool even experts. Almost every museum director—with art experts at hand—

has at some time unknowingly purchased a forgery."

"I don't understand," I tell her. "A person has to be a really good artist to be a forger. So why doesn't he exhibit his own paintings? Why copy someone else's?"

"A forger is interested in only one thing—making money. If he's still struggling to become known, he might get as little as a few hundred dollars for a painting. However, if he can come up with what passes for a Picasso or a Matisse his share of the profit could amount to hundreds of thousands of dollars. The economy is so good that the art market is booming. It's big business. More and more people are buying art as an investment."

"Wouldn't the artist want to take pride in his own work?"

Ms. Montero sighs. "Unfortunately, the forger does take pride in the fact that he's good enough to fool people and get them to part with large amounts of money."

"But that's being a thief."

"Exactly. Forgery is a crime. Gallery owners who knowingly sell forged work break the law too. They're also subject to heavy fines and imprisonment."

If people knew who owned all the valuable artworks and where they were, then they couldn't be cheated. I ask, "Isn't there some kind of an international association that lists the location of every important painting? Maybe on the Internet?"

The bell rings, and I realize I'm the only one in class not in my seat.

"No," Ms. Montero says. "The idea of a registry has been proposed, but it's always been dropped. Think about it. A list of the location of every valuable painting would be an invitation to thieves." As she picks up her roll book and pen she adds, "If your friend believes his Kupka is an original, then I'm afraid he's just one more victim of forgery."

Indignation spurts into my words. "He could sue whoever sold him a fake. He could try to get his money back. He could go to the police."

She looks at me with surprise. "Yes, he could, but most victims of forgery won't."

Halfway to my desk I turn. "Why not?"

"People who have spent a great deal of money for a painting usually brag about it and show off the painting to their associates. They don't want anyone to know they've been cheated. They don't even want to know the truth themselves."

I don't think Mr. Merson would be like that. I'm sure he'd want to know. As I sit at my desk I think about Mr. Merson as a victim, not only of a would-be murderer, but also of an art forger. Do the two tie together? And where does the file about me tie in at all?

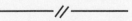

After school is over I go to Ms. Chase's art gallery. Mr. Merson has delivered some paintings to her. Has he purchased art through her gallery as well? There's one way to find out. I arrive at the Royal Heritage Gallery of Art just as Landreth is saying goodbye to two well-dressed women.

151

"Ah, our Ms. Evans," he says as they leave. "Are you still pretending to be a reporter for your school paper?"

"I wasn't trying to pretend anything," I tell him. "I just asked to see Ms. Chase."

"Are you asking again?"

"Yes, please."

He smiles. "Sorry. You're out of luck. She's not here. She'll be in New York until Wednesday."

The day after tomorrow. I don't know whether to believe him or not. Even if he's lying, what can I do about it? I refuse to give up. "Maybe I can call her," I say. "Will you tell me where she's staying?"

In a patronizing voice Landreth answers, "You might try the Pierre Hotel, although you won't find her in. Her trips to New York keep her exceedingly busy."

Okay. You win. Discouraged, I say, "Thanks," and turn away, walking to the elevators.

I wonder why I had bothered to come here. I should have gone directly to Mr. Merson instead.

As I near his house a car passes me. Gurtz with a scowl is at the wheel. Ms. Babson sits beside him, and she's crying. My heart gives a jump. *Mr. Merson's bodyguard and nurse left him alone! Is it because—?* I can't allow myself to finish the sentence.

When I reach Mr. Merson's house, I don't pull into the driveway. I park on the street, a little way back, then walk up the long drive. I'm scared. I don't know what I'm going to find out when Frederick opens the door.

I'm surprised to discover that the front door has been left ajar. I don't ring the bell. I push the door a little wider and poke my head inside. "Frederick?" My voice comes out in a whisper.

I don't want to shout, in case Mr. Merson is asleep. So I walk in, leaving the door the way I found it. I'll look through the house until I find Frederick.

The living room is empty. I hoped Mr. Merson would be there, but he isn't.

I take the hallway to the left and walk through a large dining room into a butler's pantry, and then a kitchen. There's no sign of Frederick.

There's a door to the right. With my heart once again banging in my ears, I open the door and find myself in a sitting room with a bedroom beyond. Frederick, sprawled in an armchair, is snoring loudly; a spilled glass of wine has stained the carpet next to him.

In disgust I walk out, shutting his door. I look through the other downstairs rooms. There's still no sign of Mr. Merson.

My hands are sweaty, and my heartbeat quickens. I want to yell. I could call 911, but what would I tell them? I have to find Mr. Merson myself.

It's hard to step quietly as I climb the stairs. They creak with every movement. I hold my breath and keep going.

When I reach the top I find myself on a U-shaped landing with two beautifully carved doors on each side and one in the middle. Which way should I go?

I begin with the door on the right side of the landing. I'm surprised to see that all the doors have old-fashioned, ornamental locks with keyholes. I turn the knob, and the door opens into a gorgeous bedroom with a huge four-poster bed and two deep armchairs facing a marble fireplace. The ceiling of the room shimmers with reflected sunlight from the pool below. In the bed Mr. Merson breathes rhythmically. He's sound asleep.

My fingers shake as I softly shut the door. He's all right. He's just asleep. He shouldn't have been left alone by his nurse and bodyguard, though. What was wrong with them? Where were they going? And Frederick—he's of no use to anyone.

I should leave. I have no business here. But I hope one of these doors leads to Mr. Merson's studio. I'd love to see it. Let's see . . . north light. I open the door facing the stairs and find myself in a spacious room with large windows and skylights— the perfect room for an artist. There are easels and canvases stacked against one wall, but on the other side of some low cabinets, a sturdy easel has been set up. A very large canvas rests on it. Curiosity gets the best of me. I have to look.

I tiptoe around the canvas and stare with amazement at an almost finished painting. Shocked, I gasp for breath. I know this painting. At least, I know what it's going to be. On the nearby cabinets lie enlarged, detailed photographs of the model for the painting. It's a farm scene by Chagall.

I drop to the floor and sit cross-legged as I realize what I must have suspected all along. Mr. Merson hasn't been duped by an art forger. No way. Mr. Merson *is* a forger—a very talented forger.

Through the open doorway I hear a creak on the

stair treads. There's a pause, as if someone is listening, and another stair creaks. Then another. Slowly the sound comes closer. Is it Frederick? It has to be. But what will I do if he finds me here? I crouch down, hoping the cabinets in the room will hide me.

No one comes to the studio door. Instead, I hear a nearby door open. For a while there is no sound in the house. Where is Frederick? What is he doing? Has he come to check on Mr. Merson? Not knowing, not seeing what is going on is scary. I want to run down the stairs as fast as I can, but I fight against my panic. Don't move, I tell myself. Be very quiet.

Where is Frederick?

The same door shuts softly, and in a few minutes I hear footsteps on the stairs again. This time they're running. I jump up to run too as I hear the front door slam.

But when I reach the head of the stairs I stop, my nose puckering. I recognize that smell. It's gas. And it's coming from Mr. Merson's room.

I open his door and run to the fireplace, where the gas jet is open and gas is hissing into the room. I turn off the spigot and dash to the windows, opening them wide.

"I hope you can manage to walk," I tell Mr. Merson. Using leverage, I sit him upright, being careful of his bandaged shoulder. Then I swing his legs over the edge of the bed. "Stand up," I order. "You have to."

He murmurs in the back of his throat and tries to

see me through half-lidded eyes. "I think you've been drugged," I tell him. "But I have to get you out of this room. It's still filled with gas."

Somehow we manage to make it into the hallway. I don't dare take him down the stairs, so I help him lie on the carpeting near the top. I run down the stairs, grab the phone in the living room, and call Sergeant Balker.

"I'll send an ambulance," he says. "We'll be right there. Is the person who did this still in the house?"

"It must have been Frederick," I tell him. "But I heard the door slam behind him."

Balker says something to someone. Then he gets back to me. "Some uniformed officers will get there before I do, Kristi. You can let them in. But don't let anyone else into the house."

"I won't," I tell him.

I go back upstairs and sit on the floor next to Mr. Merson. I'm still scared, and the house seems too quiet. I need someone to talk to so I won't lose my courage. Mr. Merson is still out of it. I talk to try to fight my panic.

"Your breathing seems regular," I tell him, "but you were drugged. I guess the doctors will know what to do about that. Who did this?"

I hear a tiny sound—a weird kind of moan. It comes from somewhere below me. Someone else is inside the house. I listen intently, afraid to breathe.

There's a plop, as though something has fallen. I'm so frightened that my head starts to buzz and, for a moment, I can't see.

Stop that, I tell myself.

Stumbling to my feet, I run into the studio.

Boards designed to make stretchers for the canvases are piled off to one side. I pick up a long, sturdy one and venture out into the open hallway.

Another thump from downstairs, followed by a moan.

"Stay where you are!" I yell, and raise the board as if it's a sword.

I tense, waiting for someone to answer or to appear. But no one does.

The quiet is terrifying. I can't stand it. "Where are you?" I shout. "What are you doing here?"

Again I wait, but the house is silent.

CHAPTER FIFTEEN

———— // ————

I hear a siren. It's growing louder as it comes closer. *Hurry! Hurry!* My fingers grip the board so hard they're numb.

"That's the police!" I yell, hoping I'm right. "They're coming here. They're going to get you!"

A thump from somewhere downstairs startles me. I let out a shriek and nearly drop my board.

A car squeals to a stop outside the door. Now I can hear other sirens approaching. Heavy feet run up the steps, and the door bursts open. Two police officers stare up at me.

"Help," I whisper. My knees buckle, and I sit down hard on the top step.

"Put down the board," one of them orders. His right hand rests on the gun in his holster.

I quickly throw the board to one side. "I was trying to protect Mr. Merson," I tell the officer, who runs up the stairs toward me. "Someone's down there. I don't know who it is."

The other officer disappears, then calls out, "This guy's passed out cold."

Uniformed paramedics run through the front door. Two of them head up the stairs. I squeeze against the walls of the stairwell, trying to get out of the way.

"What's with this guy's bandages?" one of them asks me.

"The Saturday before last somebody shot him in the shoulder and in the jaw," I answer. "He's recuperating."

"Recuperating? So what happened to him this time?"

"Someone turned on the gas in his room. I turned it off and opened the windows. I don't think he breathed in much of it. But he's having trouble waking up. I think he was drugged."

Sergeant Balker appears. He holds out a hand to me. "Get up, Kristi," he says. "Let's get out of their way."

As he leads me down the stairs I can see someone lying in the hallway. A paramedic is bending over him, listening to his heart with a stethoscope. "Vitals are okay," he says to his partner.

"That's Frederick!" I exclaim. "I thought he was the one who . . ."

When I don't continue, Sergeant Balker finishes the sentence. "Who turned on the gas?"

"He might have. He could be faking." I don't know why I don't trust Frederick.

Frederick struggles to sit up. "I don't need to go to the hospital," he grumbles.

"What were you drinking, Frederick?" Balker asks him.

"None of your business," Frederick grumbles.

One of the officers walks into the room from the direction of the dining room. He holds up a bottle of wine. "This is the stuff," he says. "Most of it's still in the bottle."

"Save and mark it," Balker tells him. "We'll have it analyzed." He squats down, eye-level with Frederick. "Do you usually drink on the job?"

Frederick raises his head to look at Balker. Frederick looks awful. "The wine was a gift," he says. "I poured a little into Mr. Merson's glass and helped him drink it through his straw. It looked like good wine, and I didn't want to see it go to waste. I was only going to have one glass."

I remembered the wine spilled on the carpet in his room.

"You said the wine was a gift. Who was it from?" Balker asks.

"I don't know. It was delivered." Frederick groans and rests his head on his knees.

"Take him to the hospital too," Balker tells the paramedics. "I'm guessing the wine was loaded with something. We don't know what with, but we'd better have the doctors check him out."

He says to one of the officers, "Look around for a

160

delivery slip or gift card—something that might tell us where the bottle of wine came from." Then he turns to me. "Let's sit down in the living room," Balker says. "I want to hear everything you know about what went on." He looks like Mom does when she has run out of patience. "And don't forget to tell me what you're doing here and why."

"Take him to Riverview Hospital," Frederick orders.

The paramedics look questioningly at Balker. "Yes. Go ahead. His doctor is at Riverview."

Sergeant Balker leans toward me. "Ready, Kristi?" he asks.

It only takes a few minutes, but I start at the beginning with my visit to the art gallery. I tell him everything.

When I've finished, Sergeant Balker says, "Stay put." He walks into the entry hall, and I can hear him speak to Frederick, who is loudly refusing to either walk out to the ambulance or be carried out on a stretcher. "Where did the nurse and bodyguard go?"

"Ms. Babson got an emergency phone call. Her mother had a heart attack. The doctors don't know if she'll make it. Gurtz took her to the airport."

"Which airport?"

"Bush Intercontinental . . . Continental Airlines." As Frederick goes on, his voice sounds as if he's pouting. "I told them I was perfectly capable of watching out for Mr. Merson. I've done it for years without any complaints."

"Where did the phone call come from?" Balker asks.

161

"I do remember that. Queen of the Angels Hospital in Los Angeles," Frederick answers.

"Thanks," Balker says. "Now stop creating a problem. Get out to that ambulance."

As Frederick leaves, Sergeant Balker uses his cell phone to make a call. He comes back to me and sits down on the white sofa, stretching out his legs. Staring around the room as though he's seeing it for the first time, he says, "These paintings must have cost a fortune."

"Some of them are Mr. Merson's work," I tell him. "He's an artist. I guess you know that."

"Which of all these are his paintings? Can you tell me?"

I think a moment, and then I make my decision. "I can't be sure because . . . because Mr. Merson copies paintings."

I feel sick, but I go on. "I'm pretty sure that Mr. Merson is a forger."

I point out to Sergeant Balker the signature on the Kupka painting. Then I lead him upstairs to Mr. Merson's studio and show him the "Chagall" in progress.

"Very interesting," he says. He writes something in his notebook.

As I look at the painting I begin to cry. Whatever I've built up to hold back the tears breaks loose, and they pour down my cheeks. "Please don't arrest him, Sergeant Balker," I beg. "I'm not an art expert, and I may be wrong. Just please . . . give Mr. Merson a chance to explain."

Balker's cell phone rings, and he answers. He listens a moment, then says, "Okay. Have her intercepted at Bush airport. Continental."

He snaps the phone shut, drops it into his jacket pocket, and looks at me. "Nothing's wrong with Ms. Babson's mother. The hospital didn't call. All the phone calls coming into the house today were local. Not one long-distance call."

"Do you mean somebody made up the story to frighten Ms. Babson? Why would they do a terrible thing like that to her?"

"Possibly to get her out of the house—Gurtz, too."

"But how could the person count on Gurtz taking Ms. Babson to the airport instead of Frederick?"

"Maybe it didn't matter. Gurtz may be as easily tempted by good wine as Frederick. That's a question for me to figure out."

"Meaning not me."

"Right. Meaning not you."

"About Mr. Merson," I begin, but Balker doesn't let me continue.

"Art forgery is out of my league. As homicide detectives, my partner and I will do our best to solve these attempted murders. We'll present our facts to the district attorney's office and let him come up with the art experts. He'll decide how and when to proceed with that part of the case."

"Okay," I say, feeling relieved. "That will take some time, I guess, so for now Mr. Merson will be all right."

Sergeant Balker gives me an odd look. "About as

all right as anyone can be with someone out to kill him."

I remember that I said just about the same thing to Lindy.

Balker's phone rings again. He answers, listens, then says, "Good. Bring her back."

A gruff voice calls, "What's going on?"

Sergeant Balker and I walk to the head of the stairs. We look down at Gurtz, who stands in the open doorway.

He glances warily at the policemen, then stares up at Sergeant Balker. "I shouldn't have left Mr. Merson," he says. "When the woman from the hospital called, I—"

"How do you know it was a woman?" Sergeant Balker asks.

"I answered the phone," Gurtz tells him. "She asked for Ms. Babson. I called her to the phone." His granite face seems to crumble at the edges. "I never should have trusted Frederick to do my job. If I hadn't left the house this wouldn't have happened."

Sergeant Balker's voice is so low and soft it's scary. "What do you think has happened, Mr. Gurtz?"

Gurtz looks surprised. He swallows twice. Then he says, "I don't know. But police are here in the house. You're upstairs where Mr. Merson was sleeping. Anybody can figure out that something went wrong." He glances at me, then back at Balker. "Mr. Merson is dead, isn't he?"

"No, he's not," Balker answers. "I'll be glad to answer any questions you have, Mr. Gurtz. But first

164

I have some questions to ask you about that telephone call. Go out to the kitchen, where we can talk."

As Gurtz walks away, Sergeant Balker turns to me. "Kristi, I want you to go home now. Do you need a police officer to drive you? You must be all shaken up."

"I'm okay, but will you let me know about Mr. Merson and when I can see him again?" I ask. "I told you what I thought about his work when he wasn't here to defend himself. I have to be honest with him. I want him to know what I said."

"If he's a forger, he's a criminal, Kristi. You don't owe him anything."

"There are some other things he and I need to set straight," I say.

Balker nods. "Okay. I'll let you know."

"Promise?"

"I promise."

I'm only too glad to get out of that house. I run down the street to my car and jump in. It's not until I reach San Felipe that the question hits me. Gurtz said a woman placed that fake call. Only one woman seems to be involved in Mr. Merson's life right now, and that's the gallery owner, Alanna Chase.

But Ms. Chase is in New York. Landreth said so.

A sudden thought jumps into my mind, startling me. Ms. Chase told us she was out of town—in Austin—when Mr. Merson was shot. She was out of town both of those times.

Or was she? I don't want to tell the police until I'm sure, but there's one way to find out.

CHAPTER SIXTEEN

//

I open the kitchen door, toss my backpack on the table, and reach for the telephone book. It takes a few minutes to find the number for the long-distance operator, but when I ask for the number of the Pierre Hotel in New York I get it immediately.

The hotel operator isn't as swift when I ask for Ms. Alanna Chase's room. But she finally comes back to me and says, "I'm sorry. There's no one by the name of Alanna Chase registered at the Pierre Hotel."

"Maybe she checked out early. Could you find out, please?"

It takes less than a minute before the operator returns. "I'm sorry, but Ms. Alanna Chase has not been a guest at our hotel recently."

"Thank you," I say, and hang up the phone.

I pour a glass of milk and take two oatmeal cookies out of a package in the refrigerator. Then I sit down to munch and think. Has she actually been out of town? Or has she told people she's out of town to set up an alibi for herself? Is she a suspect? Maybe.

But why would she want to kill Mr. Merson?

I remember what Ms. Montero said about people who knowingly sold forged paintings. They were guilty and could be prosecuted too.

I remember I overheard Ms. Chase telling Landreth someone was going to cooperate. She was upset. Landreth told her not to worry.

Was it Mr. Merson who was going to cooperate? And was it with the police or the FBI or whoever was involved in the sale of forgeries?

If Mr. Merson admitted his part in the forgeries, he could go to prison. If he named Ms. Chase as the dealer who sold the forgeries, she'd probably go to prison too. Did Ms. Chase try to stop him from telling the truth?

I look up the area code for Austin and go through the operator to find the number for the Four Seasons Hotel. They can't tell me when Ms. Chase checked out, or even if she stayed there. I better tell Sergeant Balker what I suspect.

It's five-thirty. Mom told me this morning to bake a chicken for dinner, but it's too early to put it into the oven. I get up from the table. I'll clean my room. No, I won't. I sit down again. I'll do my homework.

I pull my books from my backpack and open my

notebook, but the words in the textbook turn into crazy lines and squiggles that make no sense at all.

There's something I have to do, and I'm bugged by a terrible sense of urgency. Facing facts, I realize that I have to talk to Mr. Merson as soon as I can, or I may not be able to talk to him at all.

I'm not going to wait for Sergeant Balker's permission to visit Mr. Merson. There's someone else who can help me. I call Riverview Hospital and ask for Dr. Lynd.

I sigh with relief as he remembers me. "Mr. Merson's coming along fine," he says. "He's sleeping now."

"When do you think he'll wake up?"

"We'll keep him overnight and probably send him home tomorrow," he says.

Tomorrow may be too late. "Could I come to see him now?" I ask.

"Bring a good book. He might not wake up for a couple of hours."

"Thanks," I tell him.

I mix the sauce for the chicken, put it all in a baking dish, cover it, and stick it in the oven at 325 degrees. Then I dump the contents of a can of new potatoes and a can of whole string beans into a pan. Mom can heat them while she's putting the chicken on the table.

I set the table, write a note, and lay it on top of Mom's plate. *I'm going to see Mr. Merson at Riverview Hospital. I'm sorry, but I have to,* I write. That's all I need to say.

Twenty minutes later, I walk from the information desk at the hospital to Mr. Merson's room.

Gurtz sits stolidly in a chair outside the door. His eyes narrow as he peers at me, but he nods and allows me to pass.

Mr. Merson's sound asleep, just as Dr. Lynd said he would be. I pull a chair over to his bedside and sit there looking at him.

Mr. Merson has the long fingers of an artist or a magician. I glance down at my own hands. My fingers are long too.

"Which side of the family did Kristi get those long fingers from?" Aunt Darlene asked the last time she drove Grandma down to Houston for a visit. She spread out her own short, plump fingers on the table next to Mom's squared hand.

The hospital room is quiet. The closed door muffles the occasional sounds of meal carts and footsteps in the hall. I'm tired. I rest my head against the edge of the mattress and close my eyes.

I awake to the gentle touch of fingers stroking back the hair from my forehead. "Mom?" I murmur, and struggle to sit upright.

I've forgotten where I am. It takes a moment to remember. But I look into Mr. Merson's eyes. "Oh. You're awake," I say.

He points to a pad of paper and a pencil on the bedside table. I hand them to him, and he writes. "So are you."

I don't even try to smile at his teasing answer. I tell him, "Do you know what happened to you today?"

He nods and writes, "They told me you saved my life again. I'm even more in debt to you."

Leaning closer, I say, "I don't want you to be in

169

debt to me. I only want you to tell me the truth. Why have you kept the clippings and photos of me?"

For a moment Mr. Merson studies me. Then he picks up the pad and writes, "My son loved me, but he also hated me."

"Your son was supposed to be a fine person. I don't think he hated you," I tell him. "Sometimes kids get angry with their parents, but—"

Mr. Merson holds up a hand to silence me. When I stop talking, he continues to write. "Roger knew how much I wanted our family to grow. He knew I wanted a grandchild. He knew I planned to lavish love and care on that child totally from the moment it came into the world."

He hands me the page, then keeps writing. "In the resentment and anger he felt toward me, Roger exacted a terrible revenge. He became a sperm donor. He fathered children I would have no claim on, grandchildren I would never know."

The words squiggle on the page. I have trouble focusing my eyes, and my hands tremble. "Do you think I'm one of these children?" I whisper.

"Yes," Mr. Merson writes. "I know you are. Roger gave me the sketch he'd made of your mother. He told me to enjoy wondering if this was my grandchild on the way."

I struggle to make sense of what he's saying. "Wait a minute. He didn't say I *was* your grandchild. He said *if*."

"That was Roger's way of tormenting me," he writes. "I knew you had to be his child."

"Your son was *not* my father," I tell Mr. Merson. "My father's name is on my birth certificate."

He gives me a long, sad look. Then he writes, "Of course, it would be. I hired an investigator to find out as much as he could. I am familiar with Dr. Salinas's fertility clinic, as well as the circumstances of your birth at the Women's Center."

I can see that he isn't listening to me. "The names of sperm donors are kept secret," I say. "Even the women who receive the sperm don't know. No one would have given the information to your investigator. And Roger could never discover who received his sperm. That is impossible."

Mr. Merson writes, "Roger knew."

"No, he didn't. He couldn't. What you think you know is not the truth."

"Kristi," he writes, "think of what I can teach you. Think of what I can give you. You are artistic like Roger, like me. When you're ready I can give you everything."

There's a light tap at the door, and it opens. It's my mom. She doesn't come inside. She stands there looking at Mr. Merson and at me. "I'm sorry you had to go back to the hospital, Mr. Merson," she says. She moves and holds out a hand toward me. "I came to get my daughter."

I'm aware that Mr. Merson is writing again, but I don't wait to see what his message is. I get up and walk to my mother, who puts an arm around my shoulders. But as we leave the room, I stop short so quickly that we stumble. "Mom," I say, "I have to go back. Today I told Sergeant Balker . . . well, it

171

was something about Mr. Merson, and I want to be fair. I have to tell Mr. Merson what I said."

"Not now," Mom says.

Without complaint I let her guide me out of the hospital and into Dad's car.

"I'll drive," she tells me. "Your father brought me here. He's taking the other car home."

As we climb into the car I clutch her arm. "Don't start the car yet, Mom. I have to talk to you. I can't wait till we get home."

"All right, Kristi," Mom says. "Go ahead. I'm listening." She twists toward me, leaning back against her car door.

Aching at the terrible sorrow in her eyes, I start to cry, but I manage to spill out everything Mr. Merson told me.

Mom pulls a fistful of tissues from her bag and gives them to me. When I've finished mopping up, she says, "Chip . . . Roger was a tormented person. I didn't know he had such a cruel side. I'm disappointed and shocked by what he did to make his father suffer. I thought at the time he was trying to make up with his father and find peace. I was so wrong."

"But Mr. Merson believes—"

"Mr. Merson believes what he wants to believe. And just now he probably made his dream seem very real to you."

"Oh, Mom. It can't be real! I don't want it to be!" I cry. "It isn't, is it, Mom?"

"I think you know the answer to that," Mom answers.

172

"But I want *you* to say it! I want to hear it from *you!*"

"Kristi." Mom's voice is calm but full of feeling. "I could insist over and over again that Roger was not your father. I could tell you that Drew and I rejected the idea of in vitro fertilization because it involves many embryos that have to be destroyed. I could tell you that the right combination of timing and medication finally made it possible for us to conceive you. You'll have to take my word. But I can't give you absolute proof. You'll have to trust me."

Mom and Dad have dark hair. My hair is much lighter. I'm artistic and creative; while Mom and Dad are left-brained, mathematical people.

At times I've wondered about my parents, but now I have to trust. I fling myself at Mom, wrapping my arms around her, as the tears well up again. "I trust you. I believe you. Oh, Mom, I *do* believe you," I sob.

Mom holds me tightly, and I hear her crying too. "Kristi," she says, "your father and I love you with all our hearts."

CHAPTER SEVENTEEN

//

The phone rings, and I glance at the kitchen clock: 7:45 A.M. Mom and Dad have already left for work, and I have to hurry if I'm going to catch the bus for school.

But the phone blasts insistently. It's much too loud for this early hour. I gulp down the last swallow of orange juice and answer.

"He wants to see you."

I recognize the voice. "Is this Gurtz?" I ask.

"Yes. Mr. Merson wants you to come. Now."

"I can't. I have to go to school," I tell him. "I'll visit the hospital this afternoon, after school."

"He's not at the hospital. He's at home. He needs to talk to you." There's a pause, and it sounds as if Gurtz holds a hand over the speaker. He comes

174

back and adds, "He said to tell you he's running out of time."

I don't want to see Mr. Merson. I made a choice. I chose Mom and Dad. That means I pushed out of my mind forever any questions about a possible tie to Mr. Merson. But what Gurtz just said concerns me. Running out of time? I don't know what Mr. Merson means by that.

"He says come now," Gurtz repeats.

I sigh. I do owe it to Mr. Merson to let him know what I told Sergeant Balker. "Okay," I say to Gurtz. "I'll be at his house in fifteen or twenty minutes."

As soon as I hang up, I call Sergeant Balker to leave a message, but he answers the phone himself.

"Did you find out who sent the wine to Mr. Merson?" I ask him.

"Yes. Frederick told me. It's a long-standing custom for the Royal Heritage Gallery to send a bottle of expensive wine every now and then to Merson. A friendly gesture? A way of ensuring that they keep his business? Frederick claims he didn't know why."

"Maybe it was to celebrate when they sold one of Mr. Merson's paintings," I suggest.

"It's possible. Anyhow, it seems that Frederick has helped himself to some of the wine before. He knows a good thing when he sees it."

I take a deep breath and say quickly, "Sergeant Balker, I think Alanna Chase is the one who has been trying to kill Mr. Merson."

Before he can answer, I hurry to tell him what I've discovered about Ms. Chase's not being in New York at the Pierre Hotel after all. I add, "And she

175

knew that Saturdays are Frederick's days off. I think you should find her before she tries again."

Someone says something to Balker. "Right now," he answers the person. Then he says to me, "Gotta go, Kristi. You stay quiet and let us handle things. I'll get back to you." He hangs up.

Frustrated, I bang down the receiver, grab the car keys, and leave for Mr. Merson's house. Again I park out on the street and walk up the long drive.

Gurtz lets me in. "Where's Frederick?" I ask.

"Out," Gurtz answers.

"Is he feeling all right now?"

"Sure. Go on upstairs. Mr. Merson wants to see you."

I keep my eyes on the stairs. I don't dare look at the paintings as I pass them. Mr. Merson's door stands open, but I hesitate.

As Mr. Merson glances up from his chair by the fireplace, he gives a start. Then he beckons me to come in. I walk to the chair opposite him, but I don't sit down. I'd rather remain standing. Behind me I hear the door closing. Gurtz is giving us privacy. Good. That will make it easier to tell Mr. Merson what I think.

He reaches for his pad of paper and pencil, but I speak before he has a chance to write.

"I have to be honest with you," I say. "I was in your studio yesterday. I saw the Chagall you're copying. I know you're a forger."

Quickly Mr. Merson shakes his head. He writes, "I paint reproductions of beautiful paintings. I am not a forger."

I repeat what Ms. Montero had told me. "It's

176

forgery if you intend to deceive people. And people who buy the paintings think they're painted by the famous artists whose signatures are on the paintings."

"I am fortunate to be highly talented," he writes. "I know how to adopt the style and technique and spirit of a wide group of artists, such as Pissarro, Chagall, Kupka, and Picasso."

He hands me a page, then continues to write. "But I simply paint the pictures. What happens to them later is no concern of mine. If a gallery or auction house misrepresents them as having been painted by someone else, then *they* are guilty. The guilt is not mine."

"Don't you add the fake signatures?"

"What does it matter who adds them? They can be added by anyone who has access to the finished paintings."

"You're cheating people."

"On the contrary. I'm giving them what they want. Many people hang my reproductions in their homes. Even if they have doubts as to whether the paintings are originals, they pass them off as the real thing. Snob appeal is the main reason they bought the paintings."

"But there are people who buy art as an investment. You're cheating them," I insist. "You're committing a crime. You can go to prison for what you're doing."

He shakes his head, then gives me a strange smile. "Not for long," he writes. "Not if I plea-bargain."

I clamp my teeth together in frustration as I read

177

his words. I liked him at first. I sympathized with him. Now I'm disgusted. "I'm guessing that some government agency has been investigating forgeries," I tell him. "The police? The FBI? Are they coming close to discovering what you're doing? Are you going to give them the proof they want by placing all the blame on the Royal Heritage Gallery of Art?"

Mr. Merson shrugs and writes, "They took their chances."

"So Ms. Chase is guilty too," I begin, but I stop and think. What did Mr. Merson just say? *They took their chances?*

"Who is Ms. Chase's partner?" I ask Mr. Merson. I'm not surprised when he writes, "Landreth."

"Where is Ms. Babson?" I ask.

Mr. Merson shrugs. Then he writes, "She quit. She didn't return."

"Did Frederick hire Gurtz?"

Mr. Merson shakes his head.

"Did Ms. Chase?"

"Landreth," he writes.

I think of Gurtz's phone call. "Tell me, Mr. Merson, why did you send for me this morning?" I ask.

For a moment he stares at me. Then he writes, "I didn't."

"But Gurtz said you did. He called me."

Mr. Merson's eyes slowly grow wide, as we both become aware of the same thing. I probably look every bit as scared as he does. "I'm sure that Landreth has been trying to kill you—probably with Gurtz's help. I'll telephone Sergeant Balker." I

178

reach for the phone next to the bed, but the line is dead.

"Come on. Get up! Hurry!" I shout at Mr. Merson. "You and I have to get out of here!"

As he stumbles up behind me, I grab the doorknob. It doesn't turn. Gurtz has locked the door.

I run to the fireplace and pull the poker from the stand at one side. I jab as hard as I can at the door frame, trying to split the wood and release the lock. But the strong smell of smoke stops me. Wisps of smoke begin to curl under the door and into the room.

"The house is on fire!" I cry out.

Mr. Merson beats on the door with one fist.

"It's no good!" I yell at him. "Come with me! This way!"

I tug him roughly away from the door. It's the only way I can get him to move. He cries out in pain.

"I didn't mean to hurt you, but we can't go that way," I tell him. "Come with me."

I raise one of the windows. I'm not sure whether the rush of oxygen will give fuel to the fire. I just know we have to get out of that room in a hurry. "The roof of your patio is just a short drop," I tell him. "Here. I'll help you."

Pulling and pushing, I manage to get Mr. Merson out the window and down on the patio roof. There's a crackle behind me. I don't dare turn to look. As soon as he's settled, I practically dive out the window, landing beside him.

We work our way to the edge of the roof. Below

179

us is the deep end of the swimming pool. I can hear loud clacking overhead and, glancing up, see the whirling blades of a television news helicopter. And there are sirens in the distance. A neighbor must have seen and reported the fire.

I grip Mr. Merson, helping him to keep his balance. "The fire engines are coming," I say. "They'll help us." But the noise of the fire grows louder, and I can feel its heat. Bursts of black smoke swirl around us. The fire's spreading quickly. The porch roof is ablaze.

"Jump!" I shout at Mr. Merson. "Push out as you jump! The water's deep enough!"

He tries to hang back. I grab his arm and force him to look at me. His eyes droop with agony. "You won't drown," I tell him. "I'll take care of you. Jump!"

The roof shudders under our feet. He steps to the edge, pushes with his toes, and sails out over the pool.

At the same time, I hear a gunshot.

CHAPTER EIGHTEEN

—— // ——

I'm terrified that Mr. Merson has been shot, but I
have no choice. I leap out into the water too. In
the air I'm a target. In the water we'll both be un-
protected targets. But the fire gives us no choice.

I slice into the water. My feet slam against the
bottom of the pool, propelling me up. As I surface I
gulp for air, twisting to find Mr. Merson.

He's close to me, fighting the water, trying with
one hand to stay afloat.

"Lie back!" I yell as I come up behind him and
support his back. "Float!"

He obeys me, although he's sputtering water and
it must be hard for him to swallow or breathe. I slip
one arm across his chest and, with a sidestroke,
head for the shallow end of the pool. When we

181

reach the steps I help him sit, and I scan the water around us for signs of blood.

"Stay down!" I warn him. "I heard a shot."

"It's okay, Kristi," I hear Sergeant Balker's voice saying. "Gurtz is in custody now."

Balker runs down onto the top step. Others are with him, and I find myself being dragged out of the water.

"Get out of there fast!" someone shouts. "That roof is ready to collapse into the pool!"

Hanging on to Sergeant Balker, I run as quickly as I can. But we're only a few feet away when the roof does come down with a crashing noise. Dripping, rubbing water from my eyes, I watch Mr. Merson's house burning to the ground.

He's watching too. I ache. His beautiful art. It's gone.

I want to say something to let him know I'm sorry, but he turns to me, and I see a kind of triumph in his eyes. He points at the house, then makes a motion with his hands.

"I think," Sergeant Balker says, "Mr. Merson here believes that all the evidence is gone."

Mr. Merson looks pleased with himself.

Furious with him, I turn away to face Sergeant Balker. "But you and I are witnesses. We saw the Chagall he was copying."

"The D.A. likes more solid proof than reports that can't be verified," Balker says.

Mr. Merson actually chuckles. As I stare at him I think of all he promised me and hate the fact that I was tempted for even a moment. "You're not my grandfather," I snap. "You're a forger, a cheat, and a

182

liar. What Roger told you was not the truth. It was revenge for what you had done to him. He knew you were so caught up in lies, you wouldn't recognize another one. You'd like to control me, but I won't let you."

I pause for breath, trying to beat down the anger that flames up inside me. When I speak again, my voice is quieter and under control. "What I'm going to do is not revenge. It's a way of righting a wrong, of making you take responsibility for what you've done."

I tell Sergeant Balker, "I think you'll find evidence of forgery hanging in the living room of a Dr. Alonzo Salinas. The art experts can examine his Pissarro. I don't think Ms. Chase helped with the attempts at murder, but she may have known about them. She certainly knew she was selling forged paintings."

I turn and walk away. I do not look back at Mr. Merson. I do not care what happens to him. Sergeant Balker accompanies me to the place where I parked the car. "Will you write me a note?" I ask him. "I mean, I am really, *really* late for school."

He looks at me and grins. "I think before you go to school you've got a few things to do."

"Like call my parents," I say. "I know that."

"I meant find a towel, and deal with what's happened here."

A beach-sized bath towel appears, and another officer hands it to me. I wrap it around myself. I fight away tears. I'm swept by a sudden ache to cling to Mom and Dad and never let go.

I want to forget Mr. Merson and Roger Merson

or whatever he called himself. He may not have known who he was or wanted to be, but I know I will not try to be someone I am not. I choose to believe Mom and Dad. In my mind there's no doubt about it. I'm positive. I'm sure. I'm their daughter. I'm Kristin Anne Evans.

I am.

ABOUT THE AUTHOR

Joan Lowery Nixon has been called the grande dame of young adult mysteries and is the author of more than a hundred books for young readers, including *The Haunting*; *Murdered, My Sweet*; *Don't Scream*; *Spirit Seeker*; *Shadowmaker*; *Secret, Silent Screams*; *A Candidate for Murder*; *Whispers from the Dead*; and the middle-grade novel *Search for the Shadowman*. Joan Lowery Nixon was the 1997 president of the Mystery Writers of America and is the only four-time winner of the Edgar Allan Poe Best Juvenile Mystery Award. She received the award for *The Kidnapping of Christina Lattimore*, *The Séance*, *The Name of the Game Was Murder*, and *The Other Side of Dark*, which was also a winner of the California Young Reader Medal. Her historical fiction includes the award-winning series The Orphan Train Adventures and Orphan Train Children.

Joan Lowery Nixon lives in Houston, Texas, with her husband.